PROJECT ARMA

D1452714

OLIVER

NYSSA KATHRYN

OLIVER
Copyright © 2021 Nyssa Kathryn Sitarenos

All rights reserved.

Cover by Dar Albert at Wicked Smart Designs
Edited by Kelli Collins
Proofread by Marla Esposito

❀ Created with Vellum

She may have forgotten her past, but her past hasn't forgotten her...

Tori Blake arrives in Marble Falls with nothing. Nothing but a note in her hand and cash in her pocket. She doesn't know if those two things will be enough to get her the help she needs. She doesn't know if they'll lead her to the past she can't remember. What she *does* know is that someone is trying to kill her. If she doesn't figure out who she was, and fast, her past might not be the only thing she loses.

Former SEAL Oliver Bolton thinks he has everything he needs. His brothers, their self-defense business, and his freedom. Then he meets *her*. The beautiful brunette who steals his focus. When she leaves him with nothing but a fake number, Oliver assumes he'll never see her again. Until she shows up at Marble Protection —alone, afraid, and in need of his help.

Oliver can't lose Tori a second time. But as the couple gets closer, and her past even more so, they find themselves in a race against time to unlock Tori's secrets...before they're both just memories.

ACKNOWLEDGMENTS

Kelli, thank you for always working so hard to make these stories the best they can be.

Marla, thank you for finding the pesky mistakes that skip half a dozen re-writes and edits.

Will, thank you for your constant love and support.

Readers, you are everything. Thank you.

CHAPTER 1

*T*ori's heart drummed in her chest as she gazed up at the dark-tinted windows. The old brick facade, combined with the total lack of any signage, almost made the building look unoccupied.

Tori hadn't expected a big, glitzy "Marble Protection" sign, but she had expected *something*. Having to ask locals where the business was seemed...odd. Almost like they didn't want people to find them.

Nibbling her bottom lip, Tori watched as two women entered the building. She should go in. She knew she should. But nerves were keeping her feet rooted to the spot.

She'd arrived in Marble Falls two days ago. Today was Monday. Monday seemed a good day to start her search for answers. Wasn't Monday the day most people started stuff?

Tori looked down at the tattered piece of paper in her hand. It was all the information she had. God, it was probably the most precious thing in her possession. How sad was that.

Tori,

Last night was great. If you want to hang out again, you have my cell number, or call me at Marble Protection.

O xox.

O…

She'd read and re-read the note a hundred times, each time hoping for the same thing. Recognition. A memory. *Something.*

What did the O stand for? Owen…Oscar…Ollie…

What did he look like? Who was he to her?

Shaking her head, Tori gently folded the paper, returning it to her pocket.

The fact that she even had the note was a damn miracle. The waterproof lining of the jacket she'd been wearing saved it. It hadn't saved her from almost developing hypothermia, but it had saved the note.

Had she subconsciously known she might end up in the river? Known this note would be the only clue to who she was?

All right, O. I'm here. I hope you have some answers for me.

If he didn't…

God, she couldn't even think about that.

Exhaling, Tori headed across the road and pushed inside the self-defense and security business, stepping up to the front desk. Empty.

Okay, so the place wasn't top tier for customer service. Maybe their receptionist was on break?

Tori scanned the matted area to her left. At least a dozen women stood scattered around the large space, all wearing active wear and chatting quietly with one another.

Tapping her nails on the counter, Tori searched for a bell. Nope. No bell. Should she ask one of the women?

She was about to do just that when a tall man and a small brunette woman stepped out from the hall. If their hand-holding hadn't given away the fact that they were a couple, the way he tugged her body into his and pressed a kiss to her lips definitely did.

Cute.

A small smile stretched her lips at the way the woman's

cheeks flushed. At the way the man's eyes softened before walking across the room.

Before Tori could divert her gaze, the woman looked her way.

Crap. She'd been caught staring. Was it too late to pretend she hadn't been eyeballing them?

The woman headed Tori's way, stopping in front of her. "Hi, are you here for the lady's self-defense class?" The woman's voice was warm and welcoming. Two things Tori was in dire need of right now.

"No. I'm here..." *to find someone called O? To see if anyone knows who the heck I am?*

Good lord, she should have considered what she was going to say earlier.

The woman gave her a patient smile. "The class is free. The guys who run this place are actually doing an entire series of free self-defense classes for women. It's their way of giving back to the community."

Wow. That was nice of them.

She peered around the woman. The man was now standing with another guy. Both were equally huge and good-looking. Could one of them be O?

"You're welcome to join," the lady continued, drawing Tori's attention back to her. "If you're concerned about having no experience, you don't need to be. I'm as inexperienced as they come."

Tori had no idea whether she'd done any self-defense classes before. It was just another question she could add to the long list.

She was actually dressed in active wear today. Maybe if she stayed for the class, she might learn who this O was. Maybe O would recognize her?

Tori touched her head lightly. The wound had healed well over the last month. As long as she didn't get any head knocks...

"Okay."

The word was out of her mouth before she could overthink it. She'd just have to be careful.

"Great! I'm Maya, by the way."

Tori followed Maya to the mat area. "I'm Tori."

It was about three weeks since she'd woken from the accident, but still the sound of her name on her lips sounded strange. Almost unfamiliar.

"This is my first session," Maya said as they moved to stand with the group. "I'm dating Bodie, the cute guy up front with the dimples. He wanted me to take the class. Actually, he wanted to give me private sessions, but I asked to join a group." Maya leaned closer. "This way, if I'm bad, I might be able to fade into the background."

The way the guy kept looking at Maya, Tori doubted that would happen. "I'll probably be worse and take the attention off you anyway."

Bodie and the guy beside him turned to the group. Their biceps strained the material of their shirts. Holy heck, they looked like they could bench press three of her.

"Good morning, ladies. My name is Bodie, and this is Asher. We make up two of the eight men who run Marble Protection. We'll be alternating who runs the classes over the next few weeks. Today's session will be mostly introductory stuff. Not so physical, more boring. But don't worry, the fun stuff will come later."

Bodie winked at Maya before Asher spoke.

"Because we'll be spending the next few weeks together, we might go around and introduce ourselves and mention why we're here."

That was the only warning Tori got before Asher's eyes landed on her. Then she felt everyone else's attention swing her way.

Oh, jeez.

Tori cleared her throat, scrambling for words that didn't include amnesia and O. "My name is Tori. I'm here…" *because of a piece of paper in my pocket?* "To learn."

Okay, definitely not the most deep or intellectual answer, but it wasn't a lie.

Bodie's brows pulled together and his eyes remained fixed on her for a moment. Almost like he was trying to figure her out.

She wanted to laugh. She couldn't even figure *herself* out. He didn't stand a chance.

Asher nodded. "Great, thanks, Tori." His gaze shifted over to Maya.

One by one, the women introduced themselves. Some spent quite a bit of time talking. Far more than Tori. Not that it was hard to exceed her two seconds.

Once the group was done, Bodie and Asher spent the next twenty minutes discussing why an understanding of self-defense was important, when it should be used, and the value of assessing your surroundings.

Tori tried to focus on what they were saying, but her mind was all over the place. *Had* been all over the place since she'd woken up in that hospital bed.

She absently touched her hand to her head again. She was lucky that her hair covered the injury. It had taken a bit of practice, but she'd finally figured out how to pull it up in just the right way to hide the graze.

Her gaze flicked around the large room, searching for anything she may recognize. *Anyone* she may recognize.

Had she been here before?

"By paying attention to your surroundings, you may be able to avoid a situation that could lead to a physical altercation."

Tori frowned at Asher's words. Had *she* been paying attention to her surroundings before the bullet grazed her head and she'd fallen into the river? Could her situation have been avoided?

God, she was like an ever-flowing fountain of questions.

"Today, we're just going to focus on how to escape a wrist grab."

Tori turned back to the front as Bodie faced Asher. They

5

demonstrated the action of twisting the wrist around before shoving the attacker backward.

That didn't look too hard.

"Partner?"

Tori turned to Maya and smiled. "Sure."

"I apologize in advance if being my partner brings you unwanted attention from the guys."

Tori lifted a shoulder. "I could probably use the extra help."

Tori went first. Implementing the same actions Bodie had just demonstrated. The move felt easy to her. Almost like she'd performed it before.

When it came to be Maya's turn, the other woman took a bit longer to master the sequence. In fact, the moment they were told to speed the actions up to real time, Maya was in struggle town. Tori almost felt sorry for her when her cheeks flamed red at Bodie coming over to help for the fifth time.

After twenty minutes of practice, Tori wasn't sure Maya had completely mastered it, but the guys still called to everyone to stop.

Bodie was talking at the front when Tori felt eyes on her. It almost felt like a laser pinging her from the side.

Shifting her attention to the counter, she saw a man standing there. His entire focus was on her. He wasn't even trying to hide it.

Her heart gave a little jolt at the sight of him. He had sandy-blond hair that was cropped short, and deep green eyes. His strong jawline and day-old facial hair gave him a roughened, sexy aura.

He looked...powerful. And intense. And so damn sexy. There was a shadow of a smile on his lips.

Tori shifted her gaze back to the front and pretended she was listening to whatever Bodie was saying. She wasn't. She didn't hear a damn thing. All she wanted to do was look back at the green-eyed man.

One...two...three... She counted in her head to stop from looking back at him. When she got to ten, she slowly shifted her eyes back toward him.

Yep. Still looking at her. The man hadn't moved a muscle. He may as well be a glorious statue.

This time, she didn't look away. She couldn't. She almost felt imprisoned by the way he stared at her.

The air moved around her as people began to leave. It wasn't until she felt a light touch on her arm that she finally looked away from him.

"It was really nice to meet you, Tori." Maya smiled, dropping her hand from her arm. "The next class is on Thursday. I'll see you then?"

Would she? Probably. Tori had nowhere else to be. "It was nice to meet you, too. I'll see you Thursday."

Maya's smile widened before she moved away.

When Tori turned back to the man, she almost jumped out of her skin. He was no longer standing by the counter. He was less than a foot away. Touching distance. And Lord Almighty, did he smell good.

"I see you couldn't stay away, Tori."

The devastatingly good-looking man knew her. That was good. It also made her skin tingle. "I guess not."

Even if she wasn't here for a purpose, she could see how this man would draw her back.

He nodded toward the class that had just finished. "You took the class I told you about."

What would he do if she told him she had absolutely no recollection of that conversation?

Freak out? Think she was nuts? It didn't matter. She wouldn't be telling him. Not yet, anyway. Not when someone had just tried to kill her. She needed to get a better understanding of who this guy was first.

"You made it sound so appealing."

A small frown marred his brows, as if he didn't quite buy what she'd just said. "Are you passing through town for work again?"

No. She was passing through for answers. "I'd like to talk to you, actually."

Even if this guy wasn't O, he knew her. That was more than she'd had for the last few weeks.

He tilted his head to the side like he was trying to figure her out.

Asher walked past, giving the guy a nod. "Ax."

Ax? So this wasn't O? She couldn't help the bolt of disappointment.

"You came here to take the class and talk? With no call or prior warning?"

Yeah, that didn't sound normal.

He tilted his head to the side. "How long are you here?"

"I'm not sure, Ax."

The frown between his brows deepened.

Crap. Had she said something wrong? A nervous flutter swirled in her stomach.

"Ax?"

CHAPTER 2

*W*as the woman trying to be funny? Only Oliver's teammates called him Ax, and she knew that. They'd had a long conversation about it less than a month ago.

He studied her face, trying to find signs that she was messing with him. But she didn't look like she was joking. She looked... nervous. Unsure.

What the hell was going on here?

He'd only spent a day with Tori, but throughout that day, she'd been flirtatious and confident. The Tori in front of him looked as far from those two things as possible.

"Why'd you call me Ax?"

Tori's mouth opened and shut multiple times before she spoke. "That's...I mean, that's your name."

"That's my nickname. My name is Oliver."

There was the slightest widening of her sky-blue eyes. "Oliver." She breathed his name.

Even though he was confused as hell about what was happening, his body reacted to his name on her lips. It was like that the first time they'd met too. Immediate attraction.

9

Still, he was lost for words. Did the woman not remember his name?

It didn't seem possible. He wasn't so arrogant as to think that every single woman he'd spent time with remembered him, but it had only been a few weeks. He couldn't believe he was *that* forgettable.

Oliver stood silent for a moment, trying to figure her out. Trying and failing. He caught the multiple expressions flashing over her face. It was almost like she was seeing him for the first time.

Oliver tried for a smile. "I tried the number you gave me, but it was disconnected. I didn't think I was going to see you again."

She paused, clearly scrambling to think of a response. "I, um, lost my phone."

Oliver could sense a lie anywhere. An accelerated heart rate, the hitching of one's breath, pupils dilating...all were signs of deceit.

Most people wouldn't be able to hear the heart beating in someone's chest. With Oliver's altered DNA, he could.

What she'd just said was the truth.

Oliver wasn't sure if it was because of the vulnerability she was showing, or because he hadn't seen her in weeks, but his hand twitched to reach out and touch her. Tug her body into his, test if she'd forgotten his touch as well as his name.

A hand clamped on his shoulder, drawing him from his thoughts. "Ax, want to introduce me to your friend?"

Not really. He wanted answers. "Red, this is Tori. Tori, this is Red, but most people call him Bodie."

Bodie's smile was broad. Oliver had mentioned Tori before. Told his friend about the woman he'd spent a night with. Obviously Bodie hadn't forgotten. He reached out a hand.

"Nice to meet you." When Tori slipped her hand into his, an unfamiliar pang of jealousy shot through Oliver's chest.

Jealousy because his friend touched Tori first?

God, he really was living in the twilight zone right now.

"Nice to meet you, Tori." Bodie glanced at Oliver. "Next class starts in ten."

Oliver nodded before turning back to her. "I'm scheduled to run the next class and a couple more this afternoon." He ran a hand through his hair, suddenly frustrated by his lack of spare time. He'd rather get to the bottom of her unexpected visit.

He scanned the hall, wondering if any of his team was available to replace him.

"Oh, that's okay. Maya told me there's another class on Thursday. I can see you then. I don't want to be a hassle."

Thursday was only a couple of days away. But still... "How long are you in town for?"

"I haven't decided." Truth. "We could go for a coffee after Thursday's class?"

"Or we could go now?" Screw the class. This was more important. Asher was still around, he could take Oliver's place.

Tori eyed the exit. Now she wanted to escape? Why? She'd said she was here to see him.

"Honestly, it's okay. I'm not in any rush. Thursday's fine."

From his peripheral vision, Oliver noticed Bodie looking his way. Even from across the room, his friend could hear their conversation.

"I can at least walk you back to your hotel." He was *assuming* she was staying at a local hotel, anyway.

She was already shaking her head. "That's okay. I mean, thank you for offering. I'll see you Thursday for the next class, Oliver."

Tori offered a quick smile that didn't come close to reaching her eyes before heading out the door. He noticed that she took nothing with her. Not a bag, not even a new phone.

When Tori stepped outside, Oliver considered following. He could easily do so undetected. But she clearly didn't want his company.

"She's back."

Oliver finally took his eyes off the door to look at Bodie. His friend was standing beside him again. "I don't think she remembers me."

It sounded even stranger out loud than it had in his head.

Bodie's brows pulled together. "Wasn't it only a few weeks ago that you were together?"

"Less than a month ago." Twenty-two days, to be exact.

Bodie was silent for a moment before he threw his head back and laughed. "Maybe you just aren't that memorable."

Oliver didn't laugh. He couldn't even muster a smile. Because he knew there was something else going on. He watched as Tori disappeared down the street.

There'd been something about the look on her face that had him pausing.

Uncertainty.

It looked out of place. She'd been so damn self-assured the last time he'd seen her. She'd worn her confidence like a badge of honor.

"I'll be right back."

"Of course you will," Bodie muttered under his breath as Oliver ran outside.

TORI WRAPPED her arms around her middle as she made her way back to the motel.

He'd been right there. The only person she knew who may have any answers. Less than a foot away. Yet she hadn't asked a single question.

Why?

Because something in her gut had screamed for her to be careful. It wasn't just the suspicion in his eyes or the air of danger that surrounded him. It was something else. Something in the back of her mind that had kept her lips sealed and made her walk away.

It wasn't that she thought he was the person who'd aimed a gun at her head and sent her into the river. Figuring him out a bit more before she spilled her guts felt smart, though.

"Tori."

The sound of Oliver's voice had Tori almost tripping over her own feet. She came to a quick stop but didn't turn around straight away. Nervous tension gripped her spine.

It's okay, Tori. Be confident.

Forcing a smile to her lips, she turned. "Miss me already?"

Good. She sounded a million times more poised than she had in Marble Protection.

Just like he had inside, Oliver stepped close. So much closer than a stranger would stand. Taking up all her personal space. Then his hand went to her arm, and for the first time that morning, he touched her.

Awareness shot through her limbs.

"Are you okay?"

She frowned at his gentle words. "Of course." She fixed her gaze on his, trying to focus on anything but his touch on her arm because it was doing strange things to her insides. "I've had a long couple of weeks."

It didn't get any truer than that.

"Anything I can help with?"

Yes. I just wish I trusted you. "I'm okay. But I'm looking forward to our coffee date on Thursday."

Hopefully, by then, she'd be more prepared. Maybe the word "danger" wouldn't be flashing through her mind.

Oliver was silent for a moment. His hand still on her arm. Then he nodded. "Done."

"Great. I'll, ah, see you then, Oliver."

His thumb brushed over the bare skin of her arm, sending goose bumps to the surface. "See you then, Tori."

When his hand dropped, she swore she could still feel him.

He turned, heading back to Marble Protection. She stood there for a good twenty seconds before finally heading back to the motel.

Rest. That's what she needed. To sleep off this strange morning. To figure out what the hell she was going to do and whether she was going to take a chance on this stranger and trust him.

She needed her memories back. She'd lost every single one of them, bar a couple from her childhood. And in doing so, she didn't know who the hell she was. She'd lost her identity.

It was scary. To lose yourself. To not know how she'd ended up floating down the Colorado River or who'd shot her.

A shiver coursed down Tori's spine as she turned a corner.

The only reason she had the means to be here, to stay in a motel, was the cash that had been in her pocket. Ten thousand dollars. Who the hell put ten thousand dollars in their pocket?

Tori already knew the answer. Someone who was in trouble. Someone who was running.

Ten minutes later, she arrived at the motel. Her room was on the bottom floor at the end of the walkway. She moved inside quickly before locking the door and leaning against it.

She needed answers, and she needed them soon. Even if it meant trusting a man who could pose a huge threat.

$\mathcal{T}$ori sank lower into the tub. The warm water lapped around her like a giant soothing blanket.

Bliss. Or at least the closest she was going to get. She may not remember much about who she was, but she did know that a warm bath with a glass of wine could go a long way in soothing a scattered mind.

Her feet ached from walking around town all day. Her mind was tired from trying to ignite some sort of memory or familiarity.

She'd gained nothing new. Maybe she hadn't explored the town when she'd been here last. Maybe Oliver was the only person she'd seen and his home the only place she'd gone...if she'd gone to his home at all.

So many questions...

If it wasn't so frustrating, it would almost be funny, the things the mind hung on to. She remembered her favorite foods, in particular burritos and wine...yes, she was classifying wine as a food group. She remembered math, spelling, direction... procedural memory, as the doctor had described it. She even had fragments of memories from her childhood. Of playing in parks, sitting in classrooms, running around ovals...

All of which told her diddly-squat about who she was today.

"Who are you, Tori no-last-name?" She lifted her glass and swirled the contents. "Are you an adventurer? An academic?"

Maybe she was a historian who spent every spare moment at a museum.

Ha, she doubted it. She certainly hadn't gravitated toward any art or sculptures that she'd occasionally passed in the last few weeks.

Why was it that meaningless memories stayed with her, yet the recent memories, the ones which would tell her something about the person she was today, were gone?

Not just gone. Stolen. Taken from her and buried somewhere she couldn't find.

She sipped the wine, letting the fruity flavors of the Shiraz soothe her frayed insides.

The worst part was that when she'd woken up in the hospital with no recollection of her name, address, or loved ones, people had told her someone would be looking for her. Someone would contact the hospital or police when she didn't return home. When she missed work or yoga class.

That's why she'd remained in a motel near the hospital all those weeks. She'd been waiting for someone to collect her.

Well...they hadn't.

Sighing, she placed the glass back on the edge of the bath.

No one's missing you, Tori. Not a single soul.

And with no ID, her whole life was the cash and note in her pocket.

Tori poked a foot out of the tub and studied her tattoo. A half sun sat on the inside of her left ankle.

When had she gotten the tattoo? *Why* had she gotten it? Was there a story behind it? A meaning? Did someone else have the other half?

Gah. Why didn't she remember?

Tomorrow. Tomorrow she would spend time with Oliver after the class. She would not let his overwhelming good looks and silky-smooth voice turn her to mush. And she would not let the danger that surrounded him frighten her off.

He had to be a good guy. Why else would she have kept his note? She needed to trust herself.

Plus, he hadn't followed her back to her motel and tried to kill her the other day. That's what the bad guy would have done. Right?

Tori continued to study the tattoo on her ankle. Leaning forward, she brushed her finger over the outline of the sun.

Suddenly, something flashed through her mind. A memory. Of a woman laughing. A woman with big blond curls and a huge smile.

The water whooshed around Tori as she shot into a sitting position. She scrunched her eyes shut, trying to picture the woman's eyes...the rest of her face...anything.

But she went blank. The memory disappeared as quickly as it had come.

It's fine. A memory is a memory.

It was a start. A connection to who she was. Maybe next time she'd remember her face. A name.

Tori was just leaning back when a loud bang sounded from the wall that connected her room to the one next door. Rolling her eyes, she ignored it.

This was the cheapest motel in Marble Falls. All she had was cash, and cash runs out. Who knew how long it would be before she had more money?

She'd assumed the place would be okay, seeing as it was in Marble Falls. The town wasn't exactly a place of high crime. And most people at the motel *did* seem okay. Unfortunately, there was also the odd person here and there who looked rough. Like drug dealers or pimps kind of rough. And it was just her luck that some of those people had a room right beside hers.

Also, just her luck that the guy at the front desk couldn't find a new room for her.

Another bang sounded. This one louder.

Okay, relaxing bath time was well and truly over.

She'd just climbed out of the tub and wrapped a towel around her body when someone knocked on her door. It was a loud sound that reverberated through the room.

Tori remained still. Droplets of water trickled down her arms. She didn't know what the person wanted, but she *did* know there was no way in hell she was opening the door.

Another set of loud knocks.

"Hey! You got a smoke?"

A smoke? Was he serious? No, she didn't have a smoke. But even if she did, she wouldn't be opening her door and giving him one.

"Woman! I know you're in there. I need a smoke."

Go. Away. The words were on the tip of her tongue. But silence seemed smarter.

He knocked a few more times, the odd curse word filtering into his sentences. After what felt like a full minute, she finally heard his retreating footsteps.

Tori sagged. Well, if that wasn't reason enough to come clean to Oliver and figure out who she was so she could get out of this place, nothing would be.

She placed a hand to her chest, expecting her heart to be pounding. For some reason, it wasn't. Maybe the chain on her door made her feel safe?

Or maybe she was familiar with unsafe situations.

~

THE FIRST SIGN that someone was in his house was the blue sedan that sat on the street. The next was the light poking through the window blinds.

Wyatt was here. Possibly a couple more guys from his team.

His teammates were like brothers, so they could come and go as often as they liked. They each had a spare key. The question was, why were they here tonight?

Oliver parked in his driveway and headed inside. He immediately spotted Bodie lounging on the sofa, Wyatt sitting beside him. Mason stood, leaning against the wall.

There was also a fourth person in the house. Oliver could hear the person's heartbeat and their breathing coming from the kitchen. He scanned the adjoining space.

A second later, Kye walked out of the pantry, eating a bag of chips.

Oliver dropped his keys on the table beside the door. "As lovely as it is to see everyone, I feel the need to remind you that we were all together at work today. Miss me so soon?" Oliver himself had stayed late to do a workout. It wasn't unusual for him.

Wyatt leaned forward. "We want to do a background check on Tori."

Not surprising. He hadn't mentioned his strange conversation with Tori from Monday, but he knew someone who might have. He shifted his attention to Bodie. "I'm guessing I have you to thank for this?"

Bodie lifted a shoulder. "You spent a night with the woman. She's suddenly back in town, taking a class at Marble Protection, acting sketchy."

At the use of the word "sketchy," Oliver almost jumped in to defend her. He quickly gave himself a mental shake. Bodie was right. He barely knew her. She'd said she was in town to see him, then hadn't been able to get away quickly enough. It definitely *felt* like something was going on.

Mason pushed off the wall. "Doing a background check sounds like the safest thing for the team."

It was. He knew it was. But for some reason, the idea of doing one left a bad taste in his mouth. He shouldn't care. It may be an invasion of her privacy, but it was for the safety of his brothers.

"It's for the best," Kye added, shoving another chip into his mouth.

Oliver didn't know why he was hesitating. "She and I are spending time together after the class tomorrow. I'll find out what her last name is and pass on the information. You can run it through the system, Jobs."

Again, the thought of doing so didn't quite sit right in his gut. What the hell was going on with him? It had to be the vulnerability in her sky-blue eyes last Monday. They were messing with him and his damn overprotective nature.

Kye's hand stopped, chip partway to his mouth. "You didn't get a last name?"

Nope. How dumb was that?

Oliver scrubbed a hand through his hair. "I remember asking, but we got distracted by something and she never answered."

The same expression sat on each of his friends' faces. Suspicion.

"Will a coffee after class be enough?" Bodie asked.

Oliver didn't really know the woman well enough to say how long it would take to get a last name. "Don't know. Last time we were together," the only time they were together, "she didn't reveal much about herself."

Now that he thought about it, she'd revealed basically nothing.

"We could cancel the group class tomorrow and you could give her a one-on-one session," Mason suggested. "We can call around, tell everyone we've had to cancel. Tori will arrive, you tell her we didn't have a number to reach her—which we don't— so you can just instruct her yourself. That way, you have more time with her. And quite often, you can learn a great deal about a person in the way they defend themselves."

That was true. The way they flinched away from an attack or jumped into action. The speed of their heart and expression on their face.

Oliver didn't hate the idea. "Done."

Bodie smiled. "Great. We can make it up to the rest of the class by adding an extra lesson at the end of the course."

Wyatt stood. "You feeling okay with this?"

Oliver nodded. "Of course. Safety for the team is a priority." He wasn't inferring he thought she was a danger to anyone. But erring on the side of caution was always smart. Oliver shoved his hands into his pockets. "Want to stay for dinner? We can order pizza or Chinese?"

Wyatt checked his phone. "I think Quinn's actually waiting at home for me with Chinese."

"Maya's got dinner on the stove," Bodie said, standing.

"Sage asked me to pick up burgers," Mason added.

Kye shook his head. "Women come into the picture and we're all but forgotten, Ax. I'll stay for dinner."

The three guys all said their goodbyes before leaving. Kye dropped onto the couch with the bag of chips, already flicking on the TV.

Oliver grabbed his phone out of his pocket to order food, thinking about tomorrow.

Even though he'd agreed to the plan, he kind of felt like he was playing Tori. Manipulating the situation to get what he wanted. And, yet again, he wondered why he cared so much.

CHAPTER 4

*T*ori had barely stepped inside Marble Protection before she knew something was different. Where Monday, there had been the mild chatter of women, the sounds of movement, and the hustle and bustle of business, today, there was silence.

Tori shot a look over at the mat area. The room was empty.

Was the class canceled? Or maybe she'd gotten the time wrong. She could have sworn it started at ten, and it was five past...

She'd expected to walk into a class already started. She'd waited inside her motel room, listening for her neighbors to go back into *their* room. That had cost her time. Time she'd had to make up for by speed-walking here.

Now it didn't look like it mattered.

Tori shot a glance toward the door, then back to the counter. Should she just leave? Come back on Monday? And why the heck was there never anyone at the desk? Surely having someone attend the front of a business was a prerequisite for running said business?

Tori peered into the hallway, tempted to just head down there and look for someone.

That's when a door in the hall opened and Oliver stepped out.

Her mouth went dry at the sight of him in a sleeveless shirt. His impressive biceps were on display. His huge chest peeking out of the sides of the tank top.

Holy Moses, the man was ripped.

A smile stretched across his lips and she could have sworn her body heated ten degrees. He'd barely smiled on Monday. Not smiling, he was good-looking. Smiling, he was breathtaking.

"Hey there, beautiful."

Beautiful?

"Hey." She swallowed, trying to wet her dry throat. "Ah, where is everyone?"

He came to a stop in front of her, crossing those big arms over his chest. "Unfortunately, we had to cancel the class. We need two guys to run it and the others had something else pop up."

"Oh." That was disappointing. Seeing as he wouldn't be able to leave then, she was guessing that meant no coffee date. Which meant no vetting him and no amnesia confessions. It was quite the ripple effect. She attempted to cover the disappointment with a smile. "Okay. Thanks for letting me know."

"We didn't have any way to contact you, and I don't want you to have come all this way for nothing," Oliver continued. "So I've freed up the next hour to offer you a self-defense class. Hopefully, some of the guys will be back after and we can grab that coffee."

Her mouth dropped open. "Just you and me?"

His smile grew. "Just you and me, honey."

A one-on-one self-defense class with this tall, sexy, dangerous stranger? That would involve touching. Possibly lots of touching. And lots of alone time.

Oliver stepped closer, doing that thing where he invaded her personal space. "Is that okay with you?"

Was it okay? She wasn't sure. She was somewhere between running and jumping the guy. "Of course. I mean, I appreciate you setting the time aside for me. Is it okay with *you*? I don't want to interrupt if you're busy..."

"Not busy at all."

Oliver gestured toward the mat area. When Tori walked past him, he placed a hand on the small of her back. She felt it like she would if he were touching bare skin. It was electric.

How the heck had she forgotten a guy that had such a strong effect on her?

Tori hadn't brought anything with her, bar her motel key and a small amount of cash, both of which were zipped into her leggings pocket. She turned to face Oliver, attempting to push down the nerves.

"Okay, let's warm up." Oliver began by taking her through a series of warm-up activities. First was shoulder rotations. Then he systematically went through the major muscles of the body. By the end, she was warm but not tired.

She must do something to keep fit. Maybe that was why no one missed her. Did she spend all her time working out?

She almost laughed at the absurdity of that thought.

Oliver gave her a look. "What are you thinking?"

Oh, just wondering who the heck I am. "I'm wondering what you have in store for me today."

He shook his head. It was too obvious that he saw right through her. "Have you got any self-defense experience?"

"None." That she was aware of.

"I'm glad you came then. It's important that everyone has at least a basic knowledge of how to protect themselves."

Tori couldn't agree more. "I'm sure it would make walking down dark alleys a bit easier."

She was joking, of course. If she'd expected a laugh or smile from Oliver though, she didn't get either. In fact, his eyes narrowed at the comment. "Avoiding danger is always the best plan. It's important to be aware of your surroundings."

"I know. I was joking. I won't be walking down any dark alleys if I can avoid it." Sheesh, the man took his safety seriously.

"Good. I thought we'd work on escaping a hold. Specifically, when someone grabs you from behind."

Her stomach did a somersault. That meant Oliver would be putting his arms around her, didn't it? "Okay."

Her tone was much too high, and by Oliver's knowing smile, he'd heard.

"Most of the time, attackers grab people from behind because that way, the victim won't see them coming. It's also easier to drag a person backward."

"Who knew kidnappers were so strategic."

Again. Not even a hint of a chuckle.

Oliver stepped closer. Tori's heart sped up.

"What would you do if you were grabbed from behind?" he asked, his voice suddenly deepening.

"Offset their balance or cause them pain."

Tori's own eyes widened at her immediate response. Oliver's brows rose. Where the heck had that response come from?

"That's right." He studied her face. "How did you know?"

"I'm not sure."

He continued to study her for another beat before continuing. "How do you offset a person's balance?"

Step back into them. Tori bit her lip to keep from voicing the whisper in her head. "I don't know, you'll need to tell me."

She didn't know why she'd fibbed. Maybe because she'd told him she didn't have any self-defense experience, so she didn't want to come across a liar. Or maybe because the voice in her head freaked her out a little.

Now Oliver frowned.

Did the guy realize she'd lied?

"There are a couple things you can do, but we're going to

practice stepping back into the attacker and throwing them off balance. Ready to practice?"

She was careful not to react when he confirmed her thoughts. "Sure."

He took two big steps away from her. "Turn around."

"There won't be any heavy knocks, will there? Like head knocks?"

Confusion marred his features. "No. You won't get hurt, Tori. You're safe with me."

Her heart did a little flip. Wasn't that what today was about? Figuring out whether she *was* safe with him? When he said those words, gently but firmly, she couldn't help but want to trust him.

Slowly, she turned her back to him. Her heartbeat kicked up another notch in anticipation of him grabbing her.

For a moment, the room was silent. Everything still. The seconds ticked by at a snail's pace.

She didn't hear a single step before a gigantic arm wrapped around her middle and a hand covered her mouth.

From this position, she could just about feel his heart beating in his chest through her back. Oliver surrounded her. He was all she could feel.

He smelled woodsy and masculine. He smelled *good*.

Tori didn't move. She was too shocked by the way her body reacted to him. The way her blood turned molten.

"Tori..."

His voice snapped her out of her shocked state. Right. She was supposed to step back.

Oliver released her and she listened to his retreating footsteps without turning. She immediately missed his touch. Which was crazy, wasn't it?

"We'll try again."

Okay. Focus, Tori.

She waited for the attack, an odd calm settling over her body. A second passed before those same arms came around her again.

This time, she didn't freeze.

Tori stepped straight back into his body—but she didn't stop there. Almost instinctively, she spun sideways in an attempt to throw him further off balance, jabbing him in the ribs and stamping on his foot.

Offset balance, then cause pain.

The moves were strategic and familiar.

Oliver kept his balance and didn't make a sound at her attempt to hurt him. When he pulled away, his gaze returned to hers. There were questions in his eyes...lots of them.

Nervous tension steeled her spine.

"You've had self-defense training."

It would appear so. "I guess I've had a little. I, uh...forgot."

His lips thinned. Her response was weak, and they both knew it.

She expected questions to follow. Hell, she expected the man to hound her. Refuse to continue until she came clean about what she was hiding.

So she was surprised when, instead of asking anything, he returned to the corner of the room. "Again."

Tori turned around and waited for him to grab her. When he did, she repeated the move. This time faster.

Again, she was shocked by her body's ability to jump into action and know what to do.

Tori's brain may not remember anything, but her body certainly did.

Over the next hour, Oliver showed her a few more sequences to get out of similar holds. Tori reacted to each hold with the same precision and skill.

"Okay, final hold for the day. Attacker grabs you and gets you to the ground." He moved to the same corner again. "Ready?"

OLIVER INTENTIONALLY GAVE Tori no directions. He wanted to see what she'd do. He'd done it a couple of times already and she'd barely noticed. But she'd exposed herself. Demonstrated self-defense moves that would only be taught by a professional.

Something was going on here. The woman had said she had no experience, and she hadn't been lying. But she *did* have experience.

Was she a professional liar? Or was he just losing his touch?

He watched as she turned her back on him. This was the hard part...touching her while suppressing his body's reaction. She was like his damn kryptonite. He needed to snap out of it.

Oliver moved forward and wrapped his arms around her body. Then he sent them both to the floor, hitting the ground with his arm first before turning to gently hold her beneath him. He caged her soft body to the floor. Breathing her in. Waiting for her to react, while also forcing his own body to calm the hell down.

Instead of jumping into action like she had previously, other than the first time he'd attacked, she lay there. He felt a shiver course down her body. Heard the light pitter-patter of her heart take off.

"Tori..."

She didn't move. "Oliver."

Oliver leaned some of his weight to the side and turned her onto her back. The look on her face had his blood rushing south.

Desire. It clouded her eyes, taunting him. Daring him to make a move. Everything in him made him want to plant his lips to hers. To run his hands down her heated skin.

He had to pull away. Stand up. Before he did something stupid.

But Tori raised her hand and grazed his cheek with a finger. "So familiar...yet not."

What the hell did that mean?

Before he could ask, her hand lowered to his chin, grazing the area just below his lips. The touch felt right. And damn, but did it affect every inch of his body.

Without thinking, Oliver lowered his head and touched her lips with his own.

A soft hum vibrated through her chest, sending his blood soaring through his ears.

For a second, his mind screamed at him to pull away. To ask the questions that he needed answered.

But then her tongue touched the seam of his lips, coaxing its way in.

Oliver couldn't stop himself. He surrendered to the woman below him, leaning into her. Touching his chest to hers. Opening his mouth. Tasting her.

The sweetest moan rose from her throat. The fire inside him burned hotter.

This is how it had been the last time their lips met. All fire and passion. The woman had a way of affecting him on such a deep level. It was dangerous.

When their lips separated, her heavy breaths filled the air. "I remember this..." Her eyes remained closed, hands in his hair. "Your lips on mine."

Had she expected to forget?

His hand went to her face, cupping her cheek. "What's going on, Tori?"

He just wanted a straight answer. How had she forgotten his name? Why was she in Marble Falls?

"I don't know."

She spoke the truth. She really *didn't* know.

Oliver opened his mouth to ask how that was possible when the front doors of Marble Protection opened.

Cursing under his breath, Oliver jumped to his feet, pulling Tori up with him.

Luca threw him an apologetic look. "Sorry, the next class was waiting outside. We waited as long as we could."

Asher trailed in after him.

The next class? Oliver shot a look at his watch, cursing under his breath. The hour allocated for the lesson had passed; he'd gone an extra thirty minutes.

Worse, he hadn't found out a damn thing about her. Not a name or anything else of importance. He needed to have a conversation with Tori, but the more time he spent with her, the more he suspected whatever was going on went deeper than he'd originally thought.

They needed privacy for their chat. Somewhere he could talk to her and get all the answers he required. No disruptions. No time limits. A cafe would no longer do.

"Have dinner with me," he said, turning back to Tori. "Tonight. At my place."

They could chat all night if they had to.

Tori nibbled on her bottom lip. Fuck. Even that small action had his blood pumping.

"You don't want to go for a coffee?"

"The guys might need my help," he lied. "But I do want to spend more time with you today." That part wasn't a lie.

"Okay."

Okay? He didn't know why, but he'd thought she might need convincing. "Great. Seven o'clock work?"

"Seven sounds good. Can you write your address on a piece of paper for me?"

She'd been to his place, but he supposed that was easy enough to forget. "Do you have a phone yet? I can put it in." He remembered she'd mentioned losing hers.

She hesitated. "I haven't replaced it yet."

"It's your lucky day then. We happen to have an old company cell we were about to get rid of. You can borrow it. I'll grab it for you."

She opened her mouth, presumably to refuse, but he was already heading toward the office.

The phone wasn't actually an old one they were about to chuck. It was a backup phone. And, just like all the others, it had a tracker.

Oliver didn't think Tori would leave town without telling him, but the phone would be a safety net in case he was wrong. He couldn't let her leave without knowing what was going on.

When he returned with the phone, Tori was shaking her head. "I can't take your phone."

He quickly typed his address into the notes before pressing it into her hand. "We don't need it, you do. And having a phone is a safety precaution. I feel better knowing you have a way to contact people."

She remained still for a beat before nodding. "Okay."

"Good. If you need to contact me, my number is under Ax. I can pick you up if it's easier?"

"Oh, no. It's fine. I'll come to you," she answered quickly. A bit too quickly. "Thank you for the lesson, Oliver. I'll see you tonight."

Then she left. Leaving him with more questions than ever.

CHAPTER 5

*T*ori should have let him pick her up. What was the saying? Hindsight is twenty-twenty? Yeah, her lack of hindsight was biting her in the butt now.

She hadn't wanted the guy to see the cheap accommodations she was staying in. Or her lack of possessions if he'd come inside.

But now, she was once again hiding out in her room, waiting for the jerks next door to go back into theirs. It was becoming abundantly clear that it might never happen.

Maybe she should just walk out, turn the opposite direction and keep her head down. It was possible they wouldn't even notice her.

As it was, she'd already need to speed-walk to Oliver's place to avoid being late. According to Google Maps, it was a good half hour walk.

She shot a glance to the bedside table clock. Six thirty-five.

Tori waited another five minutes. Five minutes of twiddling her fingers and becoming progressively more frustrated. When the voices didn't drift away, she made her decision.

Head down. Speed-walk.

Straightening her spine, Tori took a breath of courage before stepping outside. She felt eyes on her immediately. For the first time, the men quieted.

You've got this, Tori. Head down, walk away.

She'd just locked her door when she heard him.

"Hey there, sweet cheeks. We were wondering when you'd come say hi."

Footsteps sounded, stopping right behind her.

Slowly, Tori turned to face him. The guy was tall but thin. Lines around his eyes were visible but she was thinking they were more from substance abuse than aging. "I'm just leaving."

Tori went to take a step around him, but he mirrored her movement, blocking her way. "What's the rush? Stay. Have a drink with us."

Ah, that was a big fat no. "No, thank you."

Not only did the guy remain where he was, but he also didn't seem deterred at all. In fact, his eyes slid over her face and down her body. It made her want to cross her arms and hide herself, even though little skin was showing.

Argh, the guy made her skin crawl. She should have texted Oliver and canceled.

He took a small step closer, a combination of whiskey and tobacco filling her nose. "I can make it worth your while."

"No." Her response was quick and firm, leaving no room for confusion. "Now, please move. There's somewhere I need to be."

His eyes narrowed, anger washing over his features. "That was me asking nicely. You don't want to see me ask any other way."

Well, it was sounding less and less like he *was* actually asking.

Strangely, Tori felt more annoyed than scared. Even though the guy was a good head taller and he beat her in muscle mass, she didn't feel the need to find the nearest rock to hide behind.

"And you don't want me to call the police and let them know about this little conversation. Who knows, they might even search your room and find things you don't want them to find. So, I suggest you get the hell out of my way."

The second the words left her mouth, she snapped her lips shut. Had she really just said that?

Rage contorted his features. Quicker than she'd thought he could move, he grabbed both of Tori's arms. "You should have just said yes, whore."

Again, Tori remained oddly calm. "That's the thing. I'm not a whore."

His fingers tightened, his grip punishing.

Without thinking, Tori reacted, her knee colliding with his balls.

His hand immediately released her as he bent over, crying out in pain. Before he could straighten, she grabbed his head with both hands and kneed him in the nose.

Blood spurted, splattering on her leg and dress.

His friend, who had remained silent until now, rushed forward. "You little bitch!"

His fist flew forward, but Tori was already ducking, narrowly missing the hit. While she was down, she punched him between the legs. Quickly straightening, she threw another punch, this time hitting him in the left eye.

Just like the first guy, this one howled in pain.

For a moment, she watched both men, shock zipping through her system.

Holy crap, had she really done that?

A door two rooms over opened and a group of four men stepped out. Men who, she was almost certain, were not there to save her.

"What the fuck?"

Okay, she might have some kung fu moves that her body remembered, but she had no desire to test them out on a whole group.

Spinning around, Tori unlocked the door, just managing to

get inside, close it and flick the lock before bodies collided with wood. Curse words came loud and clear, shouted from the other side.

Adrenaline rushed through her, causing her limbs to shake.

At least the nerves had kicked in now.

With numb fingers, Tori reached into her pocket and pulled out the phone, finding Ax's name on the contacts list.

When banging sounded on the glass window, Tori yelped, almost dropping the cell. Would they go so far as to break the glass? Maybe. Probably.

Tori raced into the adjoining bathroom, slamming the door shut. She clicked the lock and took a giant step back as she hit call.

He picked up immediately. "Hello."

"Oliver. It's me. Tori." She knew she was out of breath. Heck, she probably sounded like a crazed woman.

"Tori? Are you okay? What's that noise in the background?"

Oh, nothing. Just a group of lawless men, angry because I hurt their friends. "Some not so friendly guys are trying to break into my room."

Trying, and from the sounds of it, almost succeeding.

"Where are you?"

"The Duck Motel. Room eleven."

Oliver cursed across the line. Okay, so he knew the place was rough.

"I'm coming now. Make sure doors and windows are locked and see if there's anything you can use as a weapon."

"Okay." Tori hung up, already feeling better knowing that help was coming.

More banging sounded.

Jesus. How long would the door withstand their bodies ramming it? Surely someone else would hear and call the police? The guy at the front desk, at least.

Yeah, right. The guy knew they were doing god knows what

here and still turned a blind eye. It was doubtful he'd do anything to help.

Tori scanned the small bathroom. Oliver had said to look for a weapon. Unless a toilet roll counted as a weapon, there didn't appear to be much of use.

Maybe the rod that held the shower curtain? If she could remove it, that was. Stepping onto the side of the bathtub, she reached for the end of the rod.

A bang sounded from the other room. Wood hitting wall as the door slammed open.

Her breath caught in her throat. They were in her room. Now they would try to breach the bathroom. The door lock was small and old. It wouldn't hold them for long.

Oh, god. Please be close, Oliver.

She quickly disconnected the rod from the sides and pulled it down. It was too long and there were no pointy edges, but maybe, if she held it at the middle and hit them really hard, it could be useful.

A loud bang, and the lock on the bathroom door creaked from what she assumed was a shoulder hitting the wood.

Two more hits and she was sure the lock would give way. Two more hits and they'd be in.

Oliver wouldn't arrive in time. It was up to her to save herself.

Widening her stance, Tori held the rod in front of her. She waited for the attack.

Another collision with the door. More creaking of the lock.

One more...

Her fingers hurt from gripping the pole so tightly. Her breathing was labored. She watched the door, just waiting for it to burst in and the threats to enter.

Another thump echoed from the other side, but this time it was different. It wasn't a body hitting wood.

No. It sounded more like a body hitting the ground.

Then there was the sound of flesh connecting with flesh. Groans of pain.

Tori remained frozen to the spot. Her eyes still glued to the door.

More hits and groans—then silence.

Tori held her breath.

A light knock sounded on the bathroom door. So different from the bangs of moments ago.

"Honey, it's me. Oliver. Can you open the door?"

Air whooshed out of Tori's lungs. The pole slipping from her fingers, clattering to the floor. She took a moment to collect herself. To slow her breaths and straighten her spine. Then she clicked the lock that would probably have broken with another good tap and opened the door.

Oliver stood in front of her, looking just as big and dangerous as the last time she'd seen him. All the other men lay on the floor around the room, still, except for their chests, which were rising and falling.

"Are you okay?"

His words pulled her attention back to him. There was an edge to his voice, his face full of rage. A rage that would put fear into many.

"Yes." She was still coming down from the adrenaline of moments ago. But she was uninjured. And for the first time since stepping outside her motel room, she felt safe. "Thank you."

Oliver took a step forward and pulled Tori into his arms.

It took a full two seconds for her to react. To wrap her arms around his strong, warm body and sink into his powerful chest. She felt his face push into her hair.

The man calmed so much of the turmoil inside of her.

"Pack your things. You're staying with me."

His words surprised her. But at the same time, they didn't. The man had "protector" written all over him. And she was definitely a damsel in distress right now.

"Are you sure? I can move to a different motel."

She had the cash. She'd just been trying to conserve it by staying in the cheapest one in town. Big mistake.

"We can talk about it later. For now, pack your things and come to my place."

She could argue. Especially seeing as he wasn't asking so much as telling. But she was tired. And somewhere safe to stay sounded nice.

Tori moved out of his embrace, immediately missing his touch. She shoved her few belongings into her backpack, carefully stepping over the unconscious bodies as she went. "Should we call someone?" The police...an ambulance?

Oliver waited by the door. "Do you want to report this?"

"No." The word was out of her mouth quickly. Probably too quickly. Police would want her name...address...all things she didn't know.

"I'll let the guy at the desk know. I'll also let him know my team will be doing regular checks on the motel, making sure this sort of things doesn't happen again." There was a sliver of ice in his voice that had her hairs standing on end. "Are you okay to drive your car to my house?"

"I don't have a car." Tori started to throw her backpack over her shoulder, but it was taken from her fingers before she could.

His brows pulled together. "What happened to your Mazda?"

"I'm not sure." She hadn't even known she had a Mazda.

He ran a hand through his hair, clearly frustrated. As she moved ahead of him, he put a hand on the small of her back. "We'll talk at home."

Good. Tori was ready to tell him everything. And even more ready to find out what he knew.

CHAPTER 6

*O*liver waited impatiently for Tori to finish her pasta. At least one thing hadn't changed since he'd seen her last, she was still miles slower at eating than him. He'd finished his meal a good ten minutes ago and she was still going.

He'd tried to make light conversation, but everything so far had been stilted and awkward. Forced even. Too much anger was still pouring through his blood at Tori's brush with danger. If he hadn't gotten there when he had…

Oliver didn't even want to think about that. He clenched his fists under the table. He should have followed her back to her motel on Monday. At least then he would have learned that she was staying at The Duck Motel.

The place wasn't safe. It was dangerous during the day. At night, it was a damn death trap, particularly for women. The scum of the town stayed there.

Oliver could have killed the men in her room. Easily. He could have torn them apart and not batted an eyelid. They were not good people and wouldn't be missed.

He'd only just stopped himself.

When Tori's bowl was finally empty, Oliver cleared the table.

Five minutes later and he was taking Tori's small hand in his and leading her to the sofa.

He cut right to the chase. "What's going on, Tori?"

She wet her lips. "I don't remember—"

Oliver exhaled loudly, and she immediately stopped. He didn't want to hear this same line again. As avoidance tactics went, it wasn't a great one.

Tori leaned forward and touched his arm. "No, Oliver—I don't remember *anything*. Not you. Not us. Maybe one or two childhood memories...but that's it. I don't even know who I am."

Oliver studied her face, shocked.

She couldn't be telling the truth...could she?

She was.

The woman hadn't just forgotten his name. She'd forgotten almost every detail of her life. How the hell was that possible? "During our self-defense class—"

"My body reacted on autopilot, just like it did tonight when the first guy grabbed me." Oliver's jaw clenched. "I must have taken some self-defense classes or karate or something to know how to do that."

She'd definitely learned it somewhere. "What do you remember?"

She rubbed her temple. "Inconsequential moments that contain no detail of my family or where I live or anything important." She lowered her hand and shook her head. The woman looked beyond frustrated. "The doctors call it retrograde amnesia. It affects memories before the incident. They were optimistic the memory loss is temporary. That was the only good news."

Amnesia? How had she acquired amnesia between when he'd seen her last and now?

Tori answered the question without him needing to voice it. "Damage was caused to the memory-storage area of my brain when I was shot."

Oliver's entire body flinched. "Shot?"

Her mouth opened and shut, but she didn't say anything.

Oliver leaned forward and touched her arm. "Tori, did someone shoot you?"

She swallowed, and when she didn't speak for another beat, Oliver thought he might lose his mind. Then she reached for her hair. Oliver was confused about what the hell she was doing. Until he saw it.

A wound. It wasn't huge, but it was big enough to have required stitches.

"The bullet grazed your head." He breathed as he gently touched her hair around the edges.

He'd seen bullet grazes before. As far as this one went, it wasn't the worst. But the fact that she'd been shot at all...

Why?

She nodded. "Hikers found me floating in the Colorado River."

A sick feeling hit his gut hard. He didn't want to picture the woman in front of him floating unconscious in a river. Shot. Left for dead.

He had so many questions. Questions she would no longer be able to answer. More than that, he hated that she'd been hurt.

"How did you find me?"

Tori looked down at the couch as she fiddled with the edge of her shirt. "When I woke up in the hospital, all I had were my clothes. Inside my pockets, I had—"

She stopped mid-sentence.

"What was in your pockets, Tori?"

She sighed before looking up. "Ten thousand dollars and a note from you. That's why I'm here. It's how I know my name is Tori."

If the note was in her pocket, either she'd kept it there since her last visit to Marble Falls, or...

"What day were you shot?"

Her nose wrinkled, like she was trying to piece her timeline together. "Next Tuesday marks four weeks since I woke up. Doctors told me I'd been unconscious for a couple of nights."

Oliver's heart pounded loud and hard in his chest. Sunday. She'd arrived unconscious at the hospital on a Sunday.

The same Sunday he'd said goodbye to her.

For a moment, he couldn't speak.

Had his enemies tried to kill her because of him? Because she'd met him? Spent time with him?

Or maybe she'd already been connected to his enemies. Maybe their meeting wasn't as random as he'd assumed.

"What is it, Oliver?"

His blood roared loudly in his ears, but he pushed it down. He pushed it all down.

"That Sunday you were taken to the hospital is the day you left my house. I kissed you goodbye at eight o'clock that morning, and last Monday was the next time I saw you."

Her eyes widened. "So they're probably connected? Me leaving here and...someone shooting at me? That's what you're saying, isn't it?"

It was possible. So possible, his insides hurt. But he didn't want to say that out loud. He couldn't. She didn't know his past. She didn't know the enemy he and his team fought.

Or maybe she did...but she didn't remember.

Oliver avoided answering her question by asking his own. "Police never found the person who shot you, or uncovered your identity?"

She shook her head. "They searched the bank of the river, but the person was long gone. There was no evidence to track him or her. They also did a search for anyone named Tori in the area and found nothing."

From the outside, Oliver didn't react to what she said at all. Internally, his mind was reeling.

Maybe they hadn't found her because her name wasn't Tori. It was possible the woman had given him a fake name the first time they met.

He was usually good at reading people. He damn well prided himself on it. He hadn't suspected she was an enemy for a second. There'd been too much kindness in her eyes. Too much light.

Had he been wrong?

Oliver scrubbed a hand over his face. Jesus, he was confused. He'd spent a night with her. She hadn't tried to hurt him, threaten him, anything.

Tori lowered her head as she continued. "When I woke up, the doctors were sure that someone would come and claim me. A parent. Friend. Someone who discovered I was missing. Once I was released, I stayed in a motel near the hospital. Waiting. Hoping someone would come. No one ever did." Tori frowned, searching his face. "So *you* don't know? Who I am?"

Oliver wished he did. "We bumped into each other at Joan's Diner. There were no tables left and you asked if you could sit with me. We talked over our coffees. When we finished, we went for a walk. You told me you were passing through town for work, that you hadn't been to Marble Falls before, so I offered to show you around. Ended up spending the day together. You stayed here that night."

He didn't want to think about that night right now. He'd felt like he'd connected with the woman. Over one night...how crazy was that? Now he was questioning everything.

A number of emotions scattered over her face. "What did I say I did for work?"

"Whenever I asked, you changed the subject."

Damn, he was a fool. He'd let her distract him. Light touches to his arm. Leaning close and wreaking havoc on his system. He'd assumed he'd never see her again, so he hadn't pushed. Right now, he could kick his own ass for that.

"Maybe I was unemployed and too embarrassed to tell you? No boss has come forward to say I didn't show up for work."

The uncertainty in her voice had him wanting to believe that. He knew she was telling the truth about her amnesia, and she'd clearly been through a traumatic experience.

But he needed to protect himself and his brothers first.

"Maybe. I have a friend who's good at finding information. He might be able to help."

Oliver had two friends who were good, actually. Both Wyatt and Evie were great at hacking systems that most couldn't. Locating information they shouldn't.

Tori didn't look so convinced. "You think they might be able to find out who I am with just a first name?"

Oliver had no idea. "He might be able to use facial recognition. Or there might have been a missing person's report filed that you don't know about."

She looked down. "I don't know that the latter will do anything. Like I said, no employer came forward...and neither did any family."

More vulnerability. More of his instincts wanting to trust the woman, though he shouldn't.

When she blinked away the moisture in her eyes, Oliver couldn't stop himself. Reaching over, he placed his fingers under her chin, tilting her head up. He waited for her gaze to meet his. "Someone is missing you. You have touched at least one person's life in this world. Probably a hell of a lot more. I don't have to know that...to *know* that."

Some of her uncertainty lifted.

Like his hand had a mind of its own, it shifted from her chin to her cheek. Holding her. Cherishing her.

Tori leaned her face into his palm. His thumb swiped across her cheek. So damn soft.

Why did touching her feel so right? And why did he feel the need to soothe this woman, who was basically a stranger to him, when he knew damn well that she could be connected to Hylar?

"I wish I remembered you." Tori spoke the words quietly. Like she was speaking to herself.

He almost wished he could *forget* their time together. The way her body fit so perfectly against his. The soft moans that had escaped her lips...

At the sudden tightening of his body, Oliver dropped his hand and leaned back.

He couldn't touch her. She could be dangerous. Hell, she *was* dangerous. Just look at him. He was a mess around her.

Disappointment flashed over her face.

"I'll make up the spare bed for you."

She nodded. "Thank you."

He stood before he touched her again. Because another five minutes in her company and he knew he wouldn't be able to stop himself.

Yeah. She was definitely dangerous.

CHAPTER 7

"*Y*ou're a scientist?"

Tori couldn't help but be surprised. She hadn't suspected a scientist would be living in the small town of Marble Falls.

Maya smiled. "I used to work for a big pharmaceutical company in New York. That feels like a decade ago now."

"Are there any pharmaceutical companies based in Marble Falls?"

Maya chuckled. "No. I'm taking time off from working in a lab." There was some hesitancy in her voice. "There was an…incident. I need some time. Plus, Bodie needs to be here, and I want to be where he is. There aren't a lot of jobs on offer for me in Marble Falls. I miss it, but I've got a whole lifetime to work. I'm happy just *being* right now."

Tori wanted to ask about the "incident" but she didn't know the other woman well enough. This was only the second time she'd chatted with Maya.

She took a sip of the orange juice in her hand. They were at Bodie's home, sitting in his living room. Oliver was in Bodie's office with some of the other guys. They were having a team meeting, and Tori was almost certain they were talking about her.

She tried not to let that bother her.

Tori could have remained at Oliver's home, but it wasn't like she had anywhere else she needed to be. Spending time with Maya seemed the better alternative to being alone.

"You could work at the Marble Protection front desk," Tori suggested, half joking. "No one else seems to have the job."

Maya sipped her coffee. "I noticed that too. Bodie told me Evie, who's engaged to Luca, worked there for a bit, and still does the occasional shift. She's studying now. They also had Lexie, who was their main receptionist. She had a baby with Asher not that long ago and hasn't returned." Maya shrugged. "The guys have cameras up so they can see from their office when someone walks in. They can also he—"

Maya stopped before she finished what she was saying. Her mouth snapped shut.

Tori frowned. "They can also hear? Do they have an alarm system that sounds in their office?"

"Yes."

Was it just her, or had Maya answered that a bit too quickly?

"Anyway...what do you do?"

Tori nibbled on her lip, unsure how much to tell the other woman. She could always lie, but Maya would probably find out anyway. Oliver was going to tell Bodie, who would likely tell Maya.

"I can't actually remember." Maya's instant confused expression almost made Tori laugh. "I woke up almost a month ago with retrograde amnesia after suffering a head injury." She'd let Bodie fill her in on the rest.

Maya's eyes almost bugged out of her head. "Oh my god, I'm so sorry."

Tori lifted a shoulder as if it didn't bother her. As if her entire world hadn't been plunged into darkness. "That's why I'm here in Marble Falls. I had a note in my pocket from Oliver. He's going to try to help me figure out who I am."

He would no doubt be keeping an eye on her, as well. Another thing she tried to not let bother her. She'd seen the distrust in his eyes last night. The suspicion. Why, exactly, she wasn't sure. Did he suspect she'd been in town to hurt him? Why would she do that?

"So you have no idea who you are or where you live? You don't even know where your mom is?"

For some reason, when Maya said the word "mom," Tori felt a pang of pain. "No idea about any of that stuff."

Maya's brows furrowed as she clearly tried to wrap her head around what she'd just learned. Tori had been trying to wrap her head around it for the last month and had barely scratched the surface.

"That must be a bit lonely." Maya's words seemed more to herself than to Tori. Then her features cleared. "How about you come for a run with me?"

Tori chuckled. She had no idea how her amnesia and loneliness made Maya think of running. "You think that will help?"

"Yes! First, I can be great company. Take away some of that loneliness. But also, it's a great way to get your mind working. I'm not saying it will bring your memories back, but it might help?"

Tori was willing to try anything. And having a friend in town didn't sound so bad either. "Okay. Sounds great. I'm not sure how fit I am." She didn't think she was *unfit*. She'd basically run from the motel to Marble Protection the other day and hadn't been very out of breath. "Don't outrun me."

Maya was already shaking her head. "A rule amongst runners is never leave a person behind."

There was a chance Maya was making that up to help

convince her to go, but she wasn't about to argue the point. "Okay. Sounds good."

"Great! How about tomorrow morning? Oliver doesn't live far from here, so I can jog to you and then we can jog to Mrs. Potter's Bakehouse together."

Running and cake? Tori wasn't sure that was the best combination.

"We'll run to Mrs. Potter's Bakehouse, then walk home," Maya chuckled, just about reading Tori's mind.

That sounded better. "If you run every day, you must be fit." So fit that Tori was kind of hoping Maya's run to Oliver's house would tire her enough for them to be on a more even fitness level. It was entirely possible that Tori would need every advantage she could get.

Maya smiled. "I used to have a heart defect. Now that I don't, I feel like I could run all day."

Great.

The front door opened, interrupting anything Tori was about to say. A man with black hair and piercing blue eyes entered, a short blond woman by his side. In his hand were two leads, each connected to a dog.

At the sight of the dogs, Tori sucked in a quick breath. Not because she remembered anything. But because an unknown sadness suddenly filled her.

The couple stopped on the other side of the coffee table. Maya was already pushing to her feet and embracing the woman.

When Maya pulled out of the hug, she turned to Tori. "Tori, this is Mason and Sage. Guys, this is Tori."

Tori greeted the couple, trying to give them her undivided attention. It wasn't undivided though. Because she couldn't shake the sadness in her chest. Tori crouched and gave the dogs a pat, receiving plenty of licks in return.

"The mutt on the left is Nunzie, and the jumper on the right is Dizzie," Mason said.

The more she pet them, the more upset she felt. Why? Why did she feel like she could almost cry at the sight of them?

"I think I had a dog," Tori said quietly, knowing she sounded like a nutcase but unable to stop the words. "He died." Tori added the last part so quietly, no one would have heard.

Tears moistened her eyes but she madly blinked them away. She couldn't cry in front of strangers for no reason.

Standing, she took a quick step back. "They're beautiful."

Sage smiled. "They are. They make it impossible to not be a dog person."

The women started chatting but Tori was too distracted. She caught an odd look thrown her way by Mason.

Tori didn't have the memory, but she knew with absolute certainly there had been a dog in her life. And its death had been heart-wrenching.

"No memory at all? Not her name, her address, anything?" Bodie asked.

Oliver shook his head. "Nothing."

Wyatt frowned. "You're sure she wasn't…"

"Lying? I'm sure."

Wyatt didn't push it. He knew if Oliver said she wasn't lying, then she wasn't. They could all spot a lie a mile off.

Over twelve hours had passed since Tori had told him about the amnesia. About the timing of her attack. Yet Oliver was still trying to wrap his head around it.

He'd messaged his team last night and asked for a meeting this morning. Bodie, Kye, Eden, Asher, and Wyatt had made it.

"What did you learn about her the day you spent together?" Asher asked.

Ah, hell. Oliver had known this question was coming. He'd been dreading it. "Other than her first name, nothing. I didn't even get a hometown." He got none of the important stuff. Oliver leaned his elbows on the desk, running his hands through his hair. "Our conversations were light. Flirtatious. We got to know each other on a very shallow level."

"Did you sleep together?"

Trust Eden to ask the hard-hitting question. Not that he had to. They all knew the answer. They had. Oliver didn't regret it. He couldn't.

"It doesn't matter. But nothing was planned that day." Not on his end, anyway. "We had a coffee together, which became a tour of town, which became lunch..." *Etcetera, etcetera.* "I did ask her what she did for work, and she changed the subject. I didn't push."

Now that he thought about it, she'd been very good at keeping everything impersonal between them.

Wyatt tapped his fingers on the table. "It's interesting that she didn't just lie."

A heavy silence settled over the room. Oliver knew what his friend was saying. He'd actually been thinking the same thing. "You think she might have known that I could detect a lie."

It wasn't a question, but a statement.

"It's possible. The woman meets you. Spends the night with you. Then almost gets killed. Maybe..." Wyatt lifted a shoulder.

"Maybe she was here to do something but screwed up," Oliver finished for his friend. And that something had to do with him. Pain hit him hard at the idea. "I sense goodness in her."

In the way she looked at him. Spoke. Maybe he was blinded by his attraction for the woman. By the way she commanded his attention.

"I didn't sense any misgivings from her the entire time," Oliver added. "And it was she who got hurt. Not me."

"People often get hurt when they become entangled with Hylar," Luca said quietly.

Oliver could feel his defensive walls rising. Why he felt the need to defend a woman he barely knew, he wasn't sure. But he did. "I want to believe she's good. I know I have no evidence to support it. But for now, I think we should focus on learning her past, rather than hypothesizing it."

Bodie sighed. "Ax is right. We shouldn't be treating her like she's guilty of doing anything unless we know it's the case. She hasn't hurt any of us."

"We can watch her though," Eden added.

Oliver's voice hardened. "Was planning on it."

Which was true. He'd planned to watch her not only to ensure she wasn't an enemy but also to keep her safe.

"I'll get on the facial recognition," Wyatt said, already opening his laptop. "We can ask Evie to look into missing persons."

Mason walked through the door, closely followed by Nunzie and Dizzie.

Bodie frowned. "Ah, couldn't have left the mutts out there? Or, better yet, at home?"

Mason dropped the leads, the dogs moving around the room, sniffing everything. "Sage and I already told them we were spending the day together. If I'm required to work on a day off, then they can come."

Eden scoffed. "They're dogs, and you have a big-ass yard. They would have been fine."

Mason shook his head. "Nope. These guys need some people-loving. And to answer your other question, I didn't leave them in the living room because the sight of them seemed to upset Tori."

Oliver straightened. "Upset her?"

Mason's brows pulled together. "She said, 'I think I had a dog. He died.' Then she looked like she was going to cry. I think she only just managed to stop herself."

The thought of her being upset had Oliver wanting to go to her. Check that she was okay.

He gave himself a mental shake.

"Things are starting to come back to her," he mused. She'd

said she remembered their kiss yesterday, too. "We need to help her. Do what we can to figure out who she is. We also need to keep an eye on her. I don't think it will be too long before she remembers something important."

He just hoped that "something important" wasn't anything that would turn her into an enemy.

CHAPTER 8

*T*ori zipped her backpack shut. She'd only been home for five minutes. It was five minutes too long. She needed to get out. They were coming for her.

Samantha had warned her. She hadn't done what they'd asked, and now she was expendable. A loose end that needed taking care of.

What had been the best night of her life was now being followed by the day from hell. A nightmare she couldn't wake up from.

She patted the pockets of her jacket. The money and weapon were still there. Ten thousand dollars and a tranquilizer gun. Samantha had all but shoved them into her pockets, doing what she could to save her.

Tori swallowed a sob at the very real possibility that she may never see her best friend again.

She was just about to fling the bag onto her shoulder when the sound of Charlie barking from the living room stopped her. Charlie only barked when he saw something...or someone.

Tori forced calm into her body. She couldn't break down or fall apart. It was too late to run, but she refused to go down without a fight.

She turned toward the door in time to see Charlie run into the bedroom. The sound of the front door opening echoed through the house, penetrating the quiet. The safety.

Charlie took a protective stance in front of Tori. He crouched down, angry growls vibrating from his chest.

Tori's heart thumped against her ribs as a man came to stand in the doorway. A tall, muscular man. He didn't have any weapons in hand. She doubted he needed any.

A slow smile curved his lips. "Hello."

Her body wanted to crash to the floor. Run into the bathroom and use the door as a shield. She did neither. She straightened her spine and looked him dead in the eye. "Who are you?"

He took a step closer. Charlie growled louder. "That doesn't matter. What matters is that you left a job incomplete. And my boss isn't happy."

"You lied, so I pulled out."

It was as simple as that. There was no way she could have gone through with it.

"Unfortunately for you, my boss doesn't really care about the reason behind your failure. He only cares that it wasn't done."

Another step closer.

She shot a glance toward the door behind him.

His sadistic smile grew. "You can't outrun me." He tilted his head to the side. "They told you about us, didn't they? About our speed. Our strength. I'm deadlier than any other species on Earth."

Tori had been told. It was the only reason she wasn't attacking right now.

Her hand itched to grab the tranquilizer. But she had to be smart and choose her moment wisely. If she didn't, she wouldn't get another chance. "Are you trying to scare me? Wouldn't it have been easier to just burn the house down? At least then it would have looked like an accident."

"Where's the fun in that? I like to hunt my prey. Watch the panic. The fear. The pathetic desperation." The guy was sick. "And we don't care about making it look like an accident. As far as anyone's concerned, you aren't connected to us."

When the man took another step forward, Charlie lunged at him.

The guy barely spared Charlie a glance, throwing his arm out and sending her dog flying.

Charlie hit the wall hard, then fell to the ground.

Tori's world stopped. For a moment, she didn't breathe. She couldn't. His body was so still...

Her breath caught in her throat as she ran across the room. Touching him. Begging him to wake up. Charlie had become everything to her. He couldn't be dead...her heart couldn't handle it.

Panic bubbled inside her when she placed a shaking hand to his stomach. Was it rising? She couldn't tell.

A sob escaped her lips.

Oh god, please, Charlie. Take a breath. Open your eyes. Stand—

"Stupid mutt."

The man's voice sounded from right behind her. The man who easily hurt a life so precious to her. A wild anger began to rise in her chest.

"He was my mother's."

The asshole laughed. Did he find that funny?

Tori stood, angling her body to the side. The arm that was hidden reached into her pocket. Her fingers wrapping around the small gun. Her chest rose and fell in quick succession.

"Don't worry, you won't be alive long enough to mourn his death."

Pain cut through her, fueling her rage.

At the touch of his hand on her arm, Tori turned and shot.

The guy looked shocked. He reached up and yanked something out of his chest. "What the fuck?" Anger contorted his features. His hand tightened on her. Pain shot up her arm.

Wild panic coursed through her. She'd hoped it would work straight away. Samantha hadn't warned her it would take time.

The man grabbed her by the throat and slammed her against the wall. When his fingers tightened and left her with no breath, Tori grabbed at his hand, attempting to pry it away.

Her attempts were useless. The man didn't even look tired. He looked angry. Ready to kill.

Tori tried to scream. Whimper. Anything. But her throat was sealed shut.

Thin beads of sweat gathered on her temple. Consciousness began slipping away. Her heart, which had just been galloping, was already slowing.

Just as darkness was closing in on her vision, his fingers loosened, letting the first bit of air slip through her throat.

Then his entire hand dropped away, and he fell to the floor.

Tori fell beside him. Choking. Gasping for air. She remained on the ground for seconds, greedily sucking in breaths. Regaining her strength.

She had to move. She didn't have time to rest.

Pushing to her feet, she ignored the wobble. She placed one foot forward. Then another.

Tori shot a glance back at Charlie, a sob escaping her lips. If the guy woke, he'd come after her. She didn't want to leave her dog, but she had to. "I'll come back for you."

Grabbing her keys from the hallway table, Tori all but stumbled the short distance to her car.

Then she saw them. The slashed tires.

A new wave of terror rose to the surface. There were no neighbors who were within walking distance to get help. There wasn't another car in sight.

Choking back a sob, she took off toward the forested area behind the house. If she ran toward the road, she would be out in the open. This way, she would have the protection of trees. Bushes.

Her breaths came quickly. Her feet pounding the uneven ground.

Samantha had mentioned the tranquilizer would knock him out for a bit. That he'd still be weak when he woke.

God, I need you to be right, Sammy.

Tori moved her body faster than she ever thought possible. She ran through the ache in her legs. Through the burning of her throat.

The sun was just beginning to fall when she heard it. The crackle of footsteps.

He'd found her.

~

OLIVER'S EYES snapped open at the sound of Tori's labored breathing. He went from dead asleep to wide awake within seconds. A wall separated their bedrooms, but he could hear her as clearly as if she slept in the same room.

He listened for other sounds. Footsteps. A third heartbeat. He heard nothing but him and Tori.

When a small whimper sounded, Oliver was out of bed and out of his room in seconds. When he stepped into Tori's room, it was to find her alone and sleeping, but far from at peace. Small creases marred her brow. Her body jolted under the sheets like she was being attacked. When another whimper escaped her lips, Oliver was moving across the room.

Dropping to the edge of the bed, he touched her shoulder. "Tori?"

Another cry. His gut clenched at the utter despair. The terror.

Grabbing her shoulders, he shook her gently. "Tori, wake up."

Her body stilled. Her breathing shifted. Then slowly, her eyes fluttered open.

She took in her surroundings. The room was dark, almost pitch black. He could see everything, but she would barely be able to see a thing. When her eyes landed on him, she shot up into a sitting position.

Her quick movement surprised Oliver. He reached over and turned on the lamp. He expected her to talk. She remained quiet.

"Tori…"

She swallowed before dropping her head into her hands. Her body heaved a few times with heavy breaths before she spoke. "Charlie!"

There was so much sadness in that word.

"Who's Charlie, honey?"

"My dog. I…I think he was killed."

By who? Oliver needed more details.

Reaching out, he touched her knee above the blanket. Gently at first, testing her reaction. When she didn't pull away, he gave her a gentle squeeze. "Did you see Charlie in your dream?"

"Yes. He was important to me." Her words were muffled as she spoke into her hands. He caught every one of them though. "The guy threw Charlie against the wall..." A sob escaped her chest. "I think he died defending me."

When she looked up, he saw tears rolling down her face. Devastation in her eyes.

Tori's hurt made *him* hurt. He pulled her against him. Held her close.

She pressed her head into his chest. Rubbing her face like she was trying to rub away the pain. "I was in my bedroom, packing a bag. He walked in. Charlie attacked and the guy threw him into a wall. Then I shot him with a tranquilizer."

His insides jolted at the words, but he was careful not to react. Kye had been shot with a tranquilizer not long ago. One specially designed for people like them. Had she used the same weapon? If she had, how had she acquired it?

"I ran outside but my tires were slashed," she continued. "So I ran into a forested area behind my house. He followed me. Then I woke up."

Oliver began rubbing her back again. Her dream brought up more questions than answers. "Do you remember where you might live or why the guy was after you?"

"No."

Damn. They needed more.

She pushed back and rubbed her eyes. "I don't know who he was. I'm sorry I can't remember anything important."

Another tear dropped down her cheek. Oliver couldn't stop himself. Reaching up, he wiped the tear away with the pad of his thumb, wanting to soothe her pain. "I'm sorry you can't remember. It must be so hard."

"It's exhausting. Whenever something feels familiar, my brain works overtime to try to remember. And when it decides it *will* remember something, like tonight, it's the bad stuff. The scary." She shook her head. "Maybe that's what my life was..."

Oliver didn't want to believe that. "When I met you, I saw happiness in you. Energy. Vibrancy. There was good in your life."

Some of the desolation in her eyes dimmed. She wrapped her arms around him. Sank her head back into his chest.

Oliver hugged her tightly. He couldn't not.

Every new memory, everything he learned about this woman, brought up more red flags. But she also had his protective instincts working in overdrive. And he couldn't just turn that off.

CHAPTER 9

"So the guys are trailing us?" Tori shot a look over her shoulder.

Maya had told her they were, but they'd been running for a good ten minutes and Tori hadn't spotted them once.

"Yep," Maya said, not sounding the least bit short of breath. "The guys are good at staying hidden. No doubt a skill they picked up during their time as SEALs."

Tori nodded. Oliver had mentioned that him and his friends had been in a SEAL team together. There were probably hundreds of things those guys could do that normal people couldn't.

The thought of normal men doing extraordinary things brought Tori an unwelcome reminder of last night's dream. Well, less a dream and more a nightmare.

Deadlier than any other species on Earth.

Ice cooled her insides. The strength he'd possessed to hold her up against the wall, to choke her, had been unreal. Almost inhuman.

As much as she'd like to believe that her mind had made up

that part of the dream, she knew it hadn't. It was a memory. Now that she'd recaptured it, she remembered it clearly.

Tori hadn't mentioned any of that to Oliver. The oversight hadn't been intentional. She'd been focused on everything else... the memory of Charlie. Of running for her life...

"You okay?"

Tori started at Maya's question. "Yes. Sorry, was I frowning?" Or looking terrified or angry? All were very likely. "I had a coffee right before I left and it's not sitting well in my stomach."

Which wasn't a lie. The coffee was rolling around in her gut, making her feel uncomfortable. It just wasn't the main thing on her mind.

"Oh! Sorry, I didn't realize. We can walk the rest of the way if you like?"

Tori shook her head. "No, no. I'm okay. I'll let you know if it gets worse."

Tori shot another quick glance over her shoulder. Again, no sight of Oliver or Bodie.

"I had a nightmare last night." Tori wasn't sure why she'd just confessed to Maya. Maybe because she could use an ear to listen. "A memory, actually."

Maya's brows rose. "A memory that was a nightmare? Oh, that wouldn't have been nice. Want to talk about it?"

Yes. She really did. Oliver tried to hide his distrust, but Tori still saw it. Maya, on the other hand, looked at her with nothing but genuine concern.

"I was packing a bag to leave when a man entered my house. He..." Pain sliced through her chest at the memory. "He threw, Charlie, my dog, against the wall. I'm pretty sure he didn't survive. Then he tried to kill me."

Maya came to an abrupt stop, grabbing Tori's arm as she did. "Oh my god! Are you okay? I mean, I know you survived because you're standing here, but are you okay after recapturing the memory?"

"To be honest, I'm not sure. I relived the fear like it was yesterday. The heartache. I can still see the guy's eyes in my head. Feel his fingers around my neck..." Unease coursed through Tori.

Maya stepped closer, placing a hand to her shoulder. "I'm so sorry. Did you talk to Oliver? Is he taking care of you?"

His arms around her when she'd woken had made her feel safe. But this morning, he'd been distant. "I told Oliver." She nibbled on her bottom lip. "He thinks it all happened on the same day I left his house a month ago."

Maya's eyes widened. "You don't think they're connected?"

Tori rubbed her eyes. She wasn't sure *what* she thought.

There was also something else she hadn't told Oliver. A comment that her attacker had made.

You left a job incomplete.

Had Oliver been a job to her? The idea made her feel sick. How was she supposed to tell him something like that when he already didn't trust her?

"I don't know. I don't know anything. Who I am, the life I led. It's...confusing."

So unbelievably confusing.

Maya's eyes softened. "It's temporary. The not knowing, the confusion. At some point, you *will* remember. And if, on the slim chance you don't remember *everything*, you'll remember enough that you won't feel this way forever."

Temporary. That made it sound a little more bearable. She could live with temporary confusion. Temporary frustration.

What if she didn't like what she learned though?

She pushed that thought down. She didn't have the energy to pay it the attention it deserved right now.

"Thank you, Maya. I think that's exactly what I needed to hear."

An easy smile slid across Maya's lips. "You're welcome. I'm happy to be an ear to listen anytime you need to talk to someone.

I know what it's like to be new in town and not know many people."

"Thank you," she said again. And she meant it. She was so thankful for the easy friendship. And even though they hadn't known each other for long, it *did* feel like a friendship. "Now how far until we reach this amazing bakery?"

Maya chuckled. "Mrs. Potter's Bakehouse is just around the corner. You're doing really well on this run."

Tori was surprising herself. She didn't feel too out of breath. Hell, if she could hold a conversation as they ran, she was doing miles better than she'd thought.

They started jogging again.

"I'm not quite at your level, but I'm not at a dying-hedgehog level either."

Maya chuckled. "A dying hedgehog?"

"Yeah. Hedgehogs are already slow and unfit, so a dying hedgehog would be record-breaking slow and unfit."

"You're definitely not a dying hedgehog." Maya's expression became thoughtful. "Maybe a deer."

This time, it was Tori who laughed. "I'll take that. And you can be a cheetah."

"Oh, god. I wish I was that fit. Bodie's the cheetah. They all are."

Yeah, the guys at Marble Protection looked all kinds of fit. They had the builds, anyway.

They turned a corner and made it about halfway down the street when Maya came to a stop in front of a door. She pushed into the shop.

Tori hadn't even stepped inside before she was greeted with the most delicious smells. It was a mixture of dough and sugar and cinnamon that had Tori salivating.

The woman behind the counter smiled. "Maya, my favorite person. And you brought a friend to try my amazing coffee."

Maya returned the smile as they stepped up to the counter.

"Tori, this is Quinn. She's dating Wyatt. She's also Mason's sister. Quinn, this is Tori. She's staying with Oliver for a while."

Quinn perked up at that news. "So, you're the woman who's bagged one of the final two bachelors."

Ah...no. She was not. "I'm just staying with Oliver while he helps me figure out some stuff."

"Yeah, I know. He's going to help you remember your life, recapture your memories, yada yada yada. But, girl, come on, you two will end up together."

As much as she was drawn to the guy like a moth to a flame, there was a bit of a barrier between them. That barrier being her memory. Or lack thereof. "Maybe."

Being noncommittal felt like the safest option.

Quinn chuckled. "Can I make you ladies two of the best coffees in Marble Falls?"

Maya nodded.

The thought of coffee had Tori's stomach turning again. She wasn't a huge fan to begin with. "Actually, I already had a coffee today. Could I grab a juice?"

Quinn's mouth fell open. Wide open—like she'd just heard something unbelievable. It took a moment for her to turn to Maya. "Is she serious?"

"Not everyone has the same coffee addiction as you." Maya laughed, glancing at Tori. "Quinn could drink ten coffees a day—"

"Could, do, have," Quinn interjected.

Maya shook her head. "So she struggles to understand when others don't share that same compulsion."

Quinn leaned over the counter. "I make a good coffee. Used to be terrible, now it's pretty much the best in Marble Falls. *But* if you would like something else, the coffee can wait until another day."

"It will give me a reason to come in tomorrow," Tori replied, really not wanting to force another coffee into her stomach. "I'll just grab a juice today, if that's okay."

"One OJ, coming up."

A short older woman popped her head out of the door behind the counter. "All okay out here, Quinn?"

"All is great, Mrs. Potter."

Mrs. Potter scanned the area, smiling at both Maya and Tori before closing the door again.

"Sit." Quinn shooed them with her hands. "I'll get the drinks ready."

Tori headed to the table by the window with a smile on her face, grateful that the town she'd landed in had so many kind people in it.

OLIVER COULD FEEL the nervous energy bouncing off Tori. They sat in the office of Marble Protection, waiting for Wyatt and Evie.

"Relax." He whispered the word in her ear. He hated seeing her so tense and anxious. He couldn't help but want to do more to ease it.

Tori looked like she wanted to say something but snapped her mouth shut when the door opened and Wyatt and Evie walked in.

They both took seats opposite them. Wyatt nodded. "Hey, guys."

Evie smiled at Oliver before flicking her attention across to Tori. "Hi, Tori. I'm Evie."

"Hi." Tori pulled at a piece of string on her pants. He placed a hand over hers, stilling her nervous movement.

Wyatt opened his laptop. "Oliver told us about your dream. We have some pictures of people connected to our team. Enemies who might try to hurt those around us as a way to hurt *us.* We would love for you to take a look and tell us if any of them are the man you remembered attacking you."

She nodded. "I can do that."

Her hand tensed below his. He gave the back a stroke with the pad of his thumb.

Wyatt clicked a few buttons before flicking the laptop around. The picture on the screen was of their former commander, Hylar.

A muscle ticked in Oliver's jaw at the sight of him. Hylar was not only the man who'd signed them up for Project Arma, he was also the project creator. The person who sat at the top of their list of people to bring down in order to stop Project Arma.

Tori studied the picture for a moment, her brows creasing.

Was it him? Had he been the man she'd shot, then run from? Who'd shot *her*?

She shook her head. "No."

Wyatt clicked to the second image. It was of Carter, the leader of the other SEAL team who had been part of the project. His team had gone underground with Hylar when the project was shut down. He'd lost two of his men so far—Troy, who was killed by Luca, and Alistair, who died by Mason's hand. His team was down to six.

Tori shook her head. "No."

Wyatt flicked through three more images, Pete, Kip, Daniel, and Anthony. Tori said no to all of them. Oliver was beginning to wonder if maybe it wasn't one of Carter's men.

Then Wyatt flicked to the last image.

The change in Tori was immediate. Her body tensed. Her breaths shortened.

It was him.

"That's the man who was in my house."

Oliver shared a look with Wyatt.

Adrien. He was just as much of an asshole and killer as Carter. But then, they all were.

Oliver didn't know how to feel about this revelation. It was confirmed. The man who had tried to kill Tori was connected to them.

Unfortunately, that brought up even more questions. Had he tried to kill her because she'd met Oliver? Spent the night with him? Or was there another reason? A reason that, even if she remembered, she might not want to share?

CHAPTER 10

"*I*t's busy."

Busy was probably an understatement. Tori almost had to yell to be heard over the noise of the people and music. There was barely any space to move in the full bar.

"This is only my second time here. It was just as busy then too. I hear the place is popular."

Yeah, Tori could tell.

She trailed behind Maya as they moved deeper into the bar. The place had booths along opposite walls, a huge dance floor in the middle, as well as bar tables scattered around the space.

Oliver and Bodie had arrived with them, entering first. They headed toward the booth where more of their teammates sat.

Maya came to a stop beside a high circular table with two other women standing around it. One of them Tori recognized as Quinn; the other, she hadn't seen before. She had stunning red hair and a huge smile.

Quinn leaned across the table. "Where's your drink?"

"We decided to find you first," Maya said.

The redheaded woman shook her head before looking at Quinn. "Their priorities are clearly out of whack."

"I need a fresh drink anyway," Quinn said before grabbing Maya's arm. She looked to Tori. "What's your drink?"

"Whiskey sour, please."

The words were out of her mouth before she had a chance to think about them. Okay. Well, her subconscious knew her drink.

"Great."

Quinn yanked Maya toward the bar, leaving Tori with the gorgeous redhead. She chuckled. Maya was going to the bar whether she wanted to or not.

The woman smiled at Tori. "I'm Lexie, by the way. Or as some of the group now refer to me, baby mama."

"I'm Tori. Where's your little one tonight?"

"Shylah and Eden are babysitting so Mom and Dad can have a night off. Not sure how long I'll be able to keep calling him a baby though, he keeps getting bigger." An almost sad look crossed her face. "Asher's the dad. He's over there with the guys. Not sure if you've met the hunky specimen of a man?"

"I have." And he *was* quite hunky. All the guys were. But none of them commanded Tori's attention like Oliver.

"I know what you're thinking. They're all good-looking. Heck, they could star in a 'shirtless men' calendar. It would sell everywhere. The guys would become millionaires." She lifted her glass to her lips. "Not that they need the money."

She mumbled the last part before taking a sip.

"Because of their business?"

Now that she thought about it, Oliver's home was very big and new. It had to be expensive.

Lexie nodded. "Mm."

Was it Tori, or was there something strange about the way she'd answered? Noncommittally.

Evie came to stand beside Lexie. "Hey, guys."

Lexie threw her arms around the other woman in a bear hug. "My favorite bride-to-be. How are the wedding plans coming?"

Evie grinned as they separated. "Good. Now that we have a

location and a date, we can finally lock in other stuff."

Tori offered the woman a smile when she looked her way. "You're getting married?"

Evie nodded, excitement reflecting in her green eyes. "To Luca. Rocket, to the guys."

"Because he's fast," Lexie explained, shouting across the table.

Tori was almost certain they were all fast. "Do you know why they call Oliver 'Ax'?"

The women looked at each other before shaking their heads. Guess that was one Tori would need to figure out on her own.

Maya and Quinn returned with the drinks and the women began to chat. Tori found herself immersed in the conversation. The women were friendly and welcoming and made her feel comfortable without even trying. They were also entertaining. Quinn, in particular, was keeping the group laughing with her crazy stories.

Tori tried not to search out Oliver, but it was just about impossible. He was sitting in a booth not far away with five of the guys. She swore she could feel his gaze on her every so often. It was searing. The one time her gaze had clashed with his, her heart had jackhammered in her chest.

She'd had to look away.

Quinn had loaned her a short red dress for the night. It was tight, showing off every curve. She'd pulled her hair up, exposing her bare shoulders. When Tori had stepped downstairs earlier, Oliver's eyes had slid over her outfit. She could have sworn she saw them darken.

Tori's abdomen had immediately heated. She'd itched to close the distance between them. Seal her lips to his. She needed to grow some more courage first.

What would have happened if she'd done what she wanted? Would he have kissed her back?

"Let's dance."

Quinn was pulling Maya out onto the dance floor before the

words had left her mouth. Maya immediately reached back, snagging Tori's wrist. She barely had time to put her glass on the table. Then she was dancing with her new friends. Letting her body move to the up-tempo music and temporarily forgetting about everything that had been weighing on her.

The crowd was thick, and bodies were hot against her, but she found herself getting lost to the beat.

When strong hands grabbed her waist, a smile touched Tori's lips. Had Oliver been watching and decided to join her? She stepped back into him.

The smile slipped. Her body stilled. The man wasn't tall enough to be Oliver. His chest not as toned.

Tori turned around. The stranger's hands remained on her hips. He smiled down at her, his eyes glazed over. Drunk.

Tori pressed her hands to his chest, attempting to push him away, but he didn't budge. In fact, he pulled her closer. His alcohol-infused breath brushing across her face.

"Please take your hands off me," Tori said firmly.

The guy chuckled. "Come on, babe. Dance with me. I've been watching you for a while. No other guy seems to have claimed you."

Claimed her?

When his groin rubbed against her, she was moments from kneeing him between the legs. Then a hard, hot body pressed against her back.

There was no mistaking the man this time.

"She's with me. Let her go before I break your wrists, asshole." Oliver's voice sounded of barely contained rage. It was a tone she hadn't heard him use up until now.

She snuck a peek up at him, and sure enough, he looked as angry as he sounded.

The guy's hands remained on her waist for another second. She felt Oliver tense. Then her hips were released, the man's grip quickly replaced by Oliver's large, warm hands.

The guy raised his hands in surrender, stepping back. "Didn't know, buddy."

"Next time a woman says no, you step away. Got it?"

Fear flashed across the guy's face. He nodded vigorously as he took another step back. Then he was gone.

Tori turned around. "Thank you. But I had it handled, you know. The guy was a second away from a pair of bruised balls."

Oliver's gaze remained fixed over her head for a beat. Then he was looking down at her. The intensity still there but the anger easing. "Are you okay?"

She placed her hands on his chest. "I told you, I had it handled."

Instead of dropping his hands from her waist, he snaked them around her back, pulling her close. Unlike the last guy's touch, Oliver's felt intimate, making heat hum through her bloodstream.

"Broken bones probably make a bigger impression than bruised balls."

Tori rolled her eyes but couldn't help smiling. "You wouldn't really have broken his wrists."

Oliver remained silent.

Tori studied him, frowning. He wasn't serious...was he?

He looked like he was. Deadly serious.

Swallowing, she diverted her gaze back to his chest. They started to rock slowly to the music. It was at complete odds with the up-tempo song. Yet there wasn't a single part of her that wanted to change anything.

His mouth lowered to her ear. "You're killing me in that dress."

Her skin tingled in awareness. "Would it be a good death?"

"The best." He nuzzled her hair. "You smell good too. It's making me want things I shouldn't."

Like her? She wanted to ask if it would be so bad for him to have her. But indecision rendered her silent. Tori didn't know how long this version of Oliver would last. The relaxed Oliver. The Oliver who didn't hesitate to touch her and whisper sweet things into her ear. So she rested her head on his chest and enjoyed it. Enjoyed the feel of his hands on her waist. His heart beating under her ear.

She didn't know how long they'd been swaying before he broke the silence. "You do things to me that no one has done before."

She sucked in a quick breath. That was good, right?

Nibbling her bottom lip, she wanted to ask him something. Something she was pretty sure she knew the answer to but needed confirmation.

"Did we...have sex? That Saturday night?"

She was kind of hoping she was wrong. That she wasn't the kind of person who slept with a man the day she'd met him.

Casual sex...that's what it was called, right?

She felt the tiniest bit of tightening in his body. "Yes. We did."

Tori tried not to react to his words. She'd basically known as much. But still, a part of her was disappointed that she was the kind of person to do that.

She also didn't understand how she didn't remember. How had she been intimate with him, yet didn't have a single recollection of the man?

"I wish I could remember." She spoke her thoughts out loud.

"You will."

"We didn't make any plans to see each other again? After?"

Another question she knew the answer to. Still, she wanted to hear him say it. "We didn't. We swapped contact details though."

At least they'd done that much.

For the first time in a while, she looked up. Fixed her eyes on his intense green ones.

Did he know about Adrien's abilities? His extra strength and speed? If he did, he hadn't said anything. But then, neither had she.

"Has Wyatt found out anything about me?"

Like who the heck I am?

"No."

She nodded. Swallowed her disappointment. "I'm nervous."

His brows pulled together. "About not remembering everything? You will—"

"No. About remembering and not liking who I am."

Oliver stopped swaying. For a moment, he seemed to hesitate over his words. The hesitation hurt. "It'll be okay."

It'll be okay. Not "you'll like who you are" or "you have nothing to worry about".

Oliver couldn't say that…because he had the same concerns.

Tori slid her hand up his shoulder to the back of his neck. Her eyes dipped, almost not wanting to see what was in his. "Whatever happened in the past, whoever I was, there's one thing I *am* sure about. I couldn't have faked this."

This being *them*. Their chemistry. Connection.

When Oliver remained silent, she risked a peek at his face. She saw heat in his eyes. Then, to her surprise, he lowered his head and pressed his lips to hers.

The music, the people, everything that Tori had found so loud earlier, softened.

His lips moved against hers, causing her belly to do a little flop. She swayed into him, enjoying the melding of their mouths. The hypnotic passion the kiss ignited.

His tongue gently nudged her lips apart. A sigh tried to escape but got caught in her throat as they tasted each other.

Tori gripped him tighter, wishing she could stay right here, kissing this man forever.

"I can't stop wanting you," Oliver whispered when their lips separated.

She sucked in quick breaths. "I feel it too."

He pressed his temple to hers.

Tori was close to touching her lips to his again. But he

stepped back. Disappointment dropped like a weight in her gut. Oliver scrubbed a hand over his face.

Was he frustrated? Annoyed that he was attracted to her?

Tori stepped out of his embrace, his arms immediately dropping. "I'm just going to go to the bathroom." She thought it might hurt less if she broke the connection first.

It didn't.

Turning, Tori negotiated her way through the crowd.

Stupid. For a second, she actually forgot that the guy didn't trust her. Forgot that he saw her differently than she saw him.

Madly blinking the tears from her eyes, she was halfway across the room when something caught her attention. Or more accurately, *someone*.

She could only see the back of their hair, but it was familiar. So damn familiar that Tori changed direction. Increased her pace. She pushed through the crowd, all the while working hard to keep the woman in sight.

When the lady with the big blond curls stepped outside, Tori didn't think. She just followed. Needing to know whether it was someone she knew.

Samantha.

The voice was a whisper in her head. The feeling of connection and friendship she'd had with the woman strong in her heart.

Tori pushed outside. The woman was already across the parking lot. Her heels clicking against the concrete.

"Hey!" Tori called out to her, but she was too far away to hear.

She had to know. Tori ran, sprinting forward. "Samantha?"

Finally, the woman turned.

It wasn't her. Tori didn't even know what her friend looked like, but it wasn't like this woman.

Tori stopped in her tracks.

Then she heard her name shouted from the bar entrance a moment before she heard the squealing of tires.

A body collided with hers, sending her to the ground. She expected to scrape against the pavement. She expected pain.

She didn't feel any of that. She landed on a heated body.

Looking down, she saw Oliver below her.

"Oliver?" It couldn't be. His voice had been so far away moments ago.

"What the hell are you doing out here? And why are you stopping in front of moving cars?"

"I thought I saw someone familiar."

Oliver stood, pulling her to her feet with him. He wrapped a protective arm around her. "Where did he go?"

"She. She went that way." Tori pointed in the far distance. There was no one there. "I saw her blond curls and thought it was my friend. Then I saw her face and realized it wasn't her."

God, now she just felt stupid. Lots of women had long blond curls.

"Samantha."

Tori's gaze shot up to look at Oliver. "You know her?"

Please say yes. God, please let me have told you at least one thing I can use.

"Not really. You mentioned you had a friend named Samantha who had blond curls. It was in reference to wishing you had her hair."

The hope fizzled out in her. "At least I'm remembering more."

"You are." He rubbed her arm with his hand. "The breeze out here is cold. Let's get back inside."

She didn't miss how he scanned the area as they headed back into the bar.

Usually, when he touched her, she could only focus on that. On the heat he ignited inside her. This time, she was too busy thinking about how quickly he'd moved across the parking lot.

She gave him one more look before they re-entered the bar. Maybe he had secrets too.

CHAPTER 11

*T*ori studied the Colorado River. Picturing her body floating in the water, unconscious, wound to the head, wasn't comfortable.

She dragged her eyes away to look at Oliver. "So this is where the hikers found me?"

They were just outside of Buchanan Lake Village. There was nothing in the area but parkland. No buildings. No businesses. Nothing.

"According to the police report that Jobs pulled up." Oliver walked beside Tori. He placed his hand on the small of her back. Warmth penetrated through the material of her clothes to her skin. "Let's walk up the stream. See if we find anything."

Tori nodded.

When Oliver had suggested that morning that they search the area where she was found, she was totally on board. She hated days of no progress. She wasn't sure if this would help, but she was willing to give it a try.

Not that she was completely concentrating on her surroundings. Her mind was busy thinking about Oliver. About the questions that had been bugging her.

Tori shot a sideways glance his way. "Did you meet Adrien when you served?"

Oliver ran a hand through his hair. Was it just her, or did he appear uncomfortable? "Yeah. We were part of a government project together."

"What was the project?"

"To work on our recovery and learn how to train more efficiently."

She stepped over a large rock, feeling Oliver's hand slide to her elbow. She already felt a trail of goose bumps scattering across her skin from the simple touch. "Did the project achieve its goal?"

Oliver took a few seconds to answer. "It helped improve our recovery time and training. Yes."

Why did he sound so uncomfortable talking about it? "How did Adrien become your enemy?"

He brushed a hand over his frustrated expression. "Tori, I think we should concentrate on our surroundings. Me talking will only be a distraction."

He didn't need to be speaking to be a distraction. "If I was unconscious in the river, how would I remember any of this?"

"We don't know how long you were in the water. If we find the point where you fell in, you may remember."

"Shot in."

Oliver frowned. "What?"

"I didn't fall in, I was shot into the water." No memories needed to know that. "Or pushed in after I was shot. Tossed in from the riverbank."

His jaw tensed. "Fine." He turned and studied her head. "How's the wound, by the way?"

"It's fine. Almost healed." Luckily, it hadn't been too severe to begin with.

"Sorry." Oliver looked ahead again but the frown between his brows remained. "I should have asked earlier. Checked in."

She lifted a shoulder. "I'm not your responsibility."

He looked like he wanted to say something else, but didn't.

Tori sighed. The man wasn't forthcoming with his emotions, that was for sure.

The next ten minutes passed in silence. Nothing around her ignited any memories. Maybe Oliver was right. Maybe she was too distracted.

"I don't think this is going to work." Tori negotiated her way around a bush. Oliver helped by pulling the branches aside. "The doctor said that memories are fragile. My mind will remember when it's ready and there's no point in trying to force anything."

She kicked a stone and watched it ripple across the river.

"We're not trying to force anything." Oliver stepped in front of Tori as the bank between the trees and water grew narrow. "We're giving your brain a little helping hand."

Tori scoffed. Her brain felt like it needed a bit more than a helping hand. It needed a memory card inserted.

"There's a chance it could take me years to remember who I am." Jeez, if anything was going to depress her, it was that.

"It won't."

The guy was always so damn confident, wasn't he?

Tori studied his body from behind. His tight shirt stretched over his muscled back. His shorts showed enough leg to prove there wasn't a shred of fat there.

What had it felt like to be with him...to touch him?

"That weekend...was I different?"

She distinctly heard the sigh from Oliver, but he didn't stop walking. "You were the same but...a bit different, yeah."

"Different how?"

"Every so often, when you thought I wasn't watching, a contemplative expression would cross your face. A frown here and there. At the time, I thought it might have been work stress. Or stress from other parts of your life."

At the time. "Now you're not so sure?"

"Now I'm not so sure."

He didn't even try to hide his distrust this time.

"Do you think a bad past can be forgivable?"

He held a branch up for her to duck under, then he picked up his pace. "Some."

Some. Not all. He didn't need to say that last part.

So, she just had to hope she hadn't been intending to kill the guy. She didn't feel like a killer. As in, she hadn't had the urge to hurt anyone since waking in the hospital. That was good, right?

Oliver was now a fair few yards in front of Tori. *No worries, buddy. You go ahead.*

Was he trying to avoid more conversation? The idea frustrated her, and she stopped walking. He kept moving, fueling her irritation. Was it so terrible that she wanted answers about his past and whether she was forgivable?

Given the circumstances, he seemed pretty damn unreasonable. It was like he wanted to help her, but only on his terms. Well, that didn't quite work for her.

When he was a good hundred yards away and didn't look close to stopping, Tori huffed out an annoyed breath and finally started to move forward. Immediately, her foot slid off the edge of a large rock, her ankle rolling and pain running up her leg. Crying out, Tori tumbled sideways, right into the river. Her entire body dropped under the water, the chill sweeping through her system.

She was only under for a second before a hand latched onto her upper arm, ripping her clear out in one tug. She landed on the river embankment—staring at Oliver in shock.

Tori didn't pay attention to her cold limbs or the throbbing pain radiating from her ankle. Oliver had just run more than a hundred yards in under a second.

That wasn't normal. Not even close.

"Jesus, Tori, are you okay?"

Was she okay? No. She wanted to know what the hell was going on. "What are you?"

His body went unnaturally still. "What?"

"You were way ahead of me. You shouldn't have been able to pull me out of the water so quickly. And last night, the speed you had to use to get to me...that wasn't normal either."

Oliver remained still. Studying her. Probably thinking of an answer that would pass for the truth.

She wasn't in the mood for lies. She needed at least one certainty in her uncertain world right now.

AT THE SOUND of a body hitting water, Oliver whipped around to see Tori sink below the surface of the river.

He was beside her in seconds. Crouching, grabbing her arm and yanking her from the water. His jaw clenched. This was his fault. He could kick his own ass.

He inspected her body. "Jesus, Tori, are you okay?"

He shouldn't have walked so far ahead. He'd done it because touching her, even just her back, had been wreaking havoc on his system. Hell, he'd been moments away from yanking the woman into his arms. Distance to calm himself had felt necessary.

He hadn't counted on the possibility of her falling into the damn river.

"What are you?"

Oliver went still at the question. "What?"

Anger crossed her delicate features. "You were way ahead of me. You shouldn't have been able to pull me out of the water so quickly. And last night, the speed you had to use to get to me... that wasn't normal either."

He'd given himself away. Last night, and just now, he'd been careless. So anxious to save the woman, he'd put all his energy into protecting *her* rather than his secret.

Not that he would ever choose differently.

He debated over what to tell her. What kind of answer she would accept. "I was a Navy SEAL, Tori. We're trained to be fast."

Her eyes narrowed before she started pushing to her feet. Oliver grabbed her arm to help, but Tori yanked it away, almost falling over again in the process. He could have maintained his hold, but didn't want to bruise her.

"I really appreciate your help, Oliver, but what you don't seem to realize is that I'm putting my entire trust in you. Making myself vulnerable."

Oliver opened his mouth to tell her he would never hurt her, but she continued before he could.

"In my dream, Adrien told me he was more than human. Deadlier than any species on Earth. He showed me his strength. Are you like *him*?"

She knew? "Why did you keep that from me?"

"That's not an answer."

Tori turned and began to walk back the way they came. No, not walk, *limp* back the way they came. He studied her ankle, noticing for the first time how swollen it was. Slight bruising was already visible.

Jesus Christ.

"Tori..." He reached for her arm, but again, she pulled it back so hard that if he didn't let go, he was certain she'd injure herself. "You can't walk on that. I'll carry you."

She didn't stop. She didn't even turn her head. Stubborn woman.

"I don't want anything from you but the truth. And don't tell me what to do—I lost my memory, not my ability to think for myself."

"Could have fooled me," Oliver muttered loudly enough for her to hear.

Immediately, Tori spun around and limped back to him. He

had to clench his fists to stop from grabbing her and lifting her off her injured foot.

She poked her finger at his chest. "Don't. You have no idea what it's like to lose all your memories! To lose *yourself*. I'm trying to piece things together, and right now, I'm asking if you're like Adrien. I know I should have told you about him earlier. I know you don't have to tell me—"

"I am."

"No. You're not. I—"

"No." Oliver took hold of her wrist, sure that she was about to break her finger with her aggressive poking. "I *am* like him."

Christ, his team was going to kill him. But the woman already knew. Confirmation or not, she knew.

"You are?"

"Yes. And so are the guys who run Marble Protection with me."

Some of the fight left her eyes. "How is that possible?"

"That project I told you about? It was actually a cover for something else. They gave us drugs that altered our DNA and turned us into the ultimate soldiers. I'm faster and stronger than I should be. I heal faster. I see in the dark. I hear more than I should."

With every word Oliver spoke, Tori's eyes widened. "You don't look any different than a normal person."

Oliver grimaced. "It didn't change our appearance." What did she expect? Purple veins popping out of his arms and horns on his head? "Why didn't you tell me about Adrien?"

She wrapped her arms around her waist. "When I woke up, I was so fixated on Charlie and the fear of running away. Then...I don't know. I guess I was scared at what you might say. Scared at what it meant. Then when I saw how fast you were last night..." She shrugged. "I just wanted you to confirm it for me."

That's what he'd thought. It was probably why she was taking it so well.

"Did you roll your ankle on purpose? To see what I would do?"

Tori rolled her eyes but there was a ghost of a smile on her lips. "I'm not *that* desperate. If it came to it though, I might have attacked you to test how fast your reflexes were."

"Ah, yes. That might have worked. Except for the fact that even without my super-strength and speed, I'm pretty damn fast and strong."

She lifted a shoulder. "Maybe I am too."

She wasn't altered. He knew that. "You took the information really well." It wasn't every day you found out someone had altered DNA.

The small smile slipped from her lips. "Maybe it wasn't the first time I found out."

There was a beat of silence. It felt heavy. He didn't say anything because there was nothing *to* say. She wasn't talking about finding out when Adrien attacked. She was talking about finding out before that. Before she met Oliver.

Sighing, she glanced over Oliver's shoulder. "Do we keep going?"

"You're soaking wet and your ankle needs ice and elevation. I can see you're already struggling to stand. So no."

She looked down and studied her foot. "It's not too bad."

"I forgot to mention, one of my super powers is that I can spot a lie. Can I carry you back to the car?"

If she said no, he was fully prepared to throw the woman over his shoulder. She wasn't walking on that thing. No way.

She shrugged. "Of course you can. You're the strongest species on Earth."

Shaking his head, Oliver lifted Tori into his arms, liking the way she snuggled into his chest way too much.

"Are you? The strongest species on Earth?"

Oliver began walking toward the car, not caring that his shirt was getting drenched. "No idea. It hasn't been tested." Tori leaned her head on his chest. His heart gave a strange kick.

"So, Adrien's an enemy because he was part of the project?"

"Yes. His team is helping our former commander, Hylar, keep the project alive. Hylar is the co-creator of Project Arma." They'd just killed the other co-creator, Sinclair. But Tori didn't need to know every dirty detail.

She touched her hand to his chest. "I can hear the pain in your voice. I'm sorry."

His feet slowed as he glanced down at her. Real empathy showed in her eyes. It was an empathy he was certain couldn't be faked.

Yet again, he was hit with the thought that this woman couldn't have been fighting for the wrong side. Not intentionally.

"Thank you."

CHAPTER 12

"**Y**ou didn't tell me last time, did you?"

Oliver looked up from his pasta. "About my altered DNA? No. We don't tell anyone."

Of course. Media would be all over them if they found out. Not to mention the implications for the government. There'd probably be mass hysteria.

She pushed her food around her plate before sneaking another peek at Oliver from below her lashes. Christ, the man was gorgeous. A gorgeous superhuman. Veins bulged from his ginormous biceps. His jawline was so sharp, you could probably cut cheese on it.

"Why are you staring at me, Tori?"

She startled at his words.

How had he caught her? He didn't even look up.

"So…you said we slept together."

He nodded. "Yes."

"And you said it was a casual, probably-won't-see-each-other-again kind of sex?"

His jaw ticked. "I said we exchanged numbers. We didn't make any commitments to each other though." He paused. "It was a consensual decision."

Hm. "Did I initiate the sex or did you?"

Oliver placed his fork on the table. "Can we talk about something else?"

"Why? This is more important than 'are you enjoying your pasta' or any other small talk. I want to find out everything I can about the person I am. The life I led. Please, Oliver."

Oliver leaned back in his seat and ran a hand through his hair. His triceps bulged and had her mouth running dry. "You dropped a glass in the kitchen. I helped you clean it up. Then you kissed me."

So, yes. She had initiated it. She eyed the kitchen behind Oliver. "Did we have sex in there?"

He cleared his throat, looking somewhat...uncomfortable? "No. We kissed on the counter, then I carried you to the bedroom."

Her abdomen heated. Not at any memories; she had none of those. But at the crystal-clear picture he painted. "Interesting."

He frowned. "What's interesting?"

"The pieces of the Tori no-last-name puzzle." She stood, lifting her plate as she went. "You finished?"

Oliver stood too. "Sit. You need to rest your ankle."

"It's fine. Just a little bruised."

He gave her a stern look until she sat back down. He'd been making sure she remained off her foot all day. Her ankle had been thoroughly elevated and iced for hours. It honestly wasn't feeling that bad.

She watched as he took the plates into the kitchen. Rinsing them and placing them into the dishwasher. She studied the kitchen counters, wondering where exactly they'd made out. The kitchen was huge and there was plenty of counter space. There was also the big island in the center of the room.

The possibilities were endless.

"What did we eat that night?"

He returned to the table and grabbed the cups. "We ordered Chinese."

"My choice or yours?"

He chuckled. "I gave you the choice between Chinese, burgers, and pizza. You chose Chinese."

She nodded, not entirely surprised. Had he asked her that question again right now, Chinese sounded the most appealing. "What did we talk about?"

He turned the tap on. Lord Almighty. He may have been sexy sitting and eating dinner, but when the muscles in his back stretched the fabric of his shirt...the guy was irresistible.

"Go-to drink, bucket list, favorite places...normal first-date stuff."

Basically, no information that would reveal who the other person really was. "Do you remember my answers?"

"Whiskey sour, you want to float in the Dead Sea, and you love Vancouver because you went there on vacation with your mom."

Tori frowned, the odd ache in her chest at the mention of her mother yet again stirring. She pushed it aside. "The Dead Sea near Amman. A sea so salty, no living creature lives in it."

He shot her a look over his shoulder. "You remember?"

Tori rubbed her forehead. She wished. "No. Not really. Every so often, things just come to me. Tidbits of information. It's all very random." She really wished she remembered her vacation with her mother. Tori shook her head. "What were your answers?"

"Guinness, get a tattoo, and my favorite place is right here in Marble Falls with my team."

Tori smiled. The Marble Falls answer was sweet. And not a surprise. "You could get a tattoo right now." Hell, she'd hold his hand and watch the whole thing. Maybe it would remind her of the time she'd gotten her own.

"Nah. My plan is to get a tattoo when this is all over."

Her smile dimmed. Just like earlier that day, she heard the torment in his voice. It was subtle, but it was there. "What will you get?"

"A dove."

When he didn't elaborate, she had to ask. "Any particular reason?"

He put the last glass in the dishwasher before turning to face her. "Doves signify peace."

"You're not at peace right now?"

A sad smile crossed his lips. The shadows on his face darkened. "It's hard to find peace when you're constantly looking over your shoulder. Waiting for your enemy to strike. But soon."

God, it was like Project Arma affected every facet of his life. It was something that was constantly on his mind, even when it shouldn't be.

She hoped he got his peace soon.

Tori bit her bottom lip, trying to think of something to say that would lighten the mood. "I've got a tattoo."

One side of his mouth lifted. "I know. You have a half sun on your left ankle."

Man, the guy had a good memory. "Did I tell you when I got it? Or why?"

He shook his head. "I never asked."

Of course, he hadn't asked. For the same reason he hadn't tried to find out about her family or where she worked. Because they were only meant to be a one-time thing.

She watched as Oliver grabbed a towel and dried his hands. "Have you ever been in a long-term relationship?"

He shook his head. "Nope."

Nope? He didn't want to elaborate again? "Because you don't do commitment?"

He walked to the table and grabbed the salt and pepper. "Tori…"

Fine. Don't answer.

Standing, she walked slowly to the kitchen. The limp was subtle. She ignored Oliver's disapproving glare. "Was it here?" She touched the island.

Oliver's brows rose as he came to stand beside her. "What?"

"Is this where we made out?"

He blew out a long breath. Yeah, she was definitely annoying him tonight.

"It was, wasn't it?" She studied the space, trying to remember something. Anything.

Nothing came to her.

Her gaze rose back to Oliver, but instead of looking at his eyes, she paused on his lips. His perfect, oh-so-kissable lips.

What had it felt like? To make love with a man so powerful? A man she felt such a strong connection to?

A beat of silence passed before Oliver spoke. "Tori..."

He'd said her name just a moment ago...but this time, he said it differently. Almost like it pained him.

Maybe if she kissed him, here, where she'd kissed him before, she'd get another memory to add to her collection.

Tori stepped forward. "Would it be so terrible for me to kiss you right now?"

"The smart response would be yes." Oliver placed his hands on her hips, and oh lord, but did she enjoy his touch. "I've never been very smart."

Was that him giving her permission? God, he was so hard to read. Taking a chance, she splayed her hands over his chest. When Oliver didn't pull away, she slid her hands up, only stopping when they reached his neck. His eyes heated.

She was seconds away from tugging his head down and kissing him when suddenly his head lowered, and he kissed her.

There was no slow. His lips feasted on her. Passion pouring out of the man.

A deep growl vibrated through his chest. His hands moved to

her thighs, lifting her up to the counter. Her legs instinctively separated, leaving space for him to move closer. To press himself against her core.

Tori's blood roared through her veins at the feel of his hardness.

When his tongue pushed between her lips, any thoughts of trying to capture lost memories faded. *All* thoughts faded. The only thing she could think about was how damn good he felt around her.

～

THE ADDICTIVE TASTE of Tori took over. She was sweet, like honeysuckle. His blood was lava in his veins. The woman shattered his self-restraint. Pulled down the walls he'd carefully constructed and smashed them to pieces.

Tightening his grasp on her hips, Oliver tugged her closer. The hard evidence of his arousal pressing into the junction of her thighs.

His tongue explored her mouth. Dancing with hers.

Oliver lifted his hand slowly, sliding it up her waist to her breast. His fingers closed around an ample mound. He swallowed her sweet moan, loving the way she accompanied it with a small shiver.

God, the woman destroyed him.

He massaged her breast, all the while grinding his hips against her and making love to her mouth. The hard nipple in his palm called to him. Begging for attention. Using the flat of his thumb, he rubbed the sensitive peak, grazing it back and forth through her clothing.

Tori writhed in his hold, releasing sounds from her chest that would be haunting his dreams.

Her left hand lowered to his shoulder. Fingers digging into

him. Oliver switched to her other breast. Touching and playing. More sweet moans. More hip grinding.

He was just tugging up her shirt when the ringing of his phone cut through the room.

His body stilled. Their mouths still melded together, pausing in their assaults.

Tori lifted her mouth, breathing heavily. "Ignore it."

Oliver's body called for him to do just that. Screamed at him.

But the sudden interruption had pulled him back to reality. Away from the hypnotic spell this woman cast on him. If he had her again, there was a very real possibility he would want to keep her. But he didn't know who she was. Not really.

Swallowing a curse, Oliver stepped away.

The hurt expression that crossed her face had turmoil boiling in his gut. Then she crossed her arms over her chest in a protective gesture, shielding her pebbled nipples from his view, and the guilt in him intensified.

Jaw tensing, he pulled his phone from his back pocket and made his way to the study. He couldn't look at her vulnerable expression anymore. It was already tearing at his insides.

"What is it, Cage?"

"Ax. Haven't heard from you since your walk down Gorman Falls. Just wanted to check in and see if everything was okay."

Oliver sighed, dropping into his chair. Okay? Not even close. "Didn't trigger any memories." He closed his eyes, suddenly feeling both exhausted and frustrated. "I told her about our altered DNA."

There was a slight pause. "You did?"

Kye didn't sound annoyed. More bewildered than anything.

"Yeah." Oliver ran a hand through his hair. "She noticed my speed last night in the bar parking lot. Then today, she fell into the river, and I ran to tug her out without thinking. She already knew. I just confirmed it."

There'd been no point in lying. Nothing he'd be able to make up would have covered the truth. He'd already exposed himself.

He heard footsteps on the stairs outside the study.

"How'd she take it?"

"She'd seen Adrien's abilities in her dream, so she didn't run away screaming."

"Do you think she knew before?"

Even though there was nothing remotely funny about the situation, Oliver almost wanted to laugh. That very question had been playing on his mind a lot. "The more I think about it, the more I'm leaning toward yes. She was careful not to lie to me that weekend, she was attacked by Adrien... I don't know who she is. Not really."

And considering his growing feelings for the woman, that scared the hell out of him.

"We'll work this out."

But when? After he lost himself to her? After he was completely tortured by the fact he wanted her but shouldn't have her?

"If you need a break, she can stay in my guest room," Kye continued.

The idea of having Tori stay anywhere other than with him had his gut rebelling. It shouldn't. She didn't belong to him. But it did. "No, I'm okay. Maybe being here will eventually help jog some memories."

So far, it hadn't. But he couldn't lose hope.

"Okay, brother. Let me know if you need anything from me."

"Will do."

Oliver hung up just as he heard a tap switch on upstairs. It sounded like the bath. Good, she wouldn't be putting weight on her ankle.

Leaning back in his seat, Oliver scrunched his eyes shut.

Man, he'd hated seeing the look on her face when he'd pulled away. Like he'd left her exposed and vulnerable.

CHAPTER 13

*T*ori shot up into a sitting position. Her sleep-fuzzed eyes swept across the bedroom.

Samantha. She'd been right there in her dream. So close it felt as if she could touch her. She could still hear the sound of her friend's laughter. Still see the way her head was thrown back, her wild blond hair blowing in the wind.

Tori's heart pounded against her ribs. It was almost painful to remember parts of her friend, but not everything. The dream had almost felt teasing. Presenting her with oddly familiar stuff, yet never quite letting her grasp anything.

But she had recaptured one piece of information. Tori threw the sheet back and looked at her tattoo.

Samantha had half a sun tattooed on her right ankle. The other half.

They'd permanently marked their bodies together. They were close. And she knew that Samantha had a big role to play in everything that had happened to her.

Sighing, Tori dropped her head into her hands.

She was over it. So unbelievably over it. The uncertainty. The not knowing. She just wanted some concrete answers about who she was and what the heck was going on.

Throwing off the sheets, she padded out of the room and down the stairs. There was a small limp to her step, but she walked through the pain. Stepping into the dark kitchen, Tori grabbed a glass and filled it at the tap.

The quiet of the house was almost annoying. The quieter her surrounding, the louder her mind and all its questions.

Tori stared into the darkened night through the window as she took sips of water. Watched the moon reflect the tiniest hint of light.

Who was she? A teacher? A nurse? Maybe she was self-employed...

More than her profession though...was she kind? Was she respected? Did she have other friends, people she spent her Friday nights with?

Tori wasn't sure how long she stood there, watching the silent night. Wondering what kind of a life she'd forgotten. Eventually, she sighed and rinsed her glass.

Turning back toward the hall, she looked up—and her body turned to ice.

A scream got lodged in her throat at the sight of a man standing in the hallway. He was still, but so large he took up all the space. Shadows covered over his face.

Quickly, Tori reached across the counter and grabbed a knife from the block, pointing it forward.

When he took three large steps into the room, the air whooshed out of her lungs like a deflated balloon. She pressed her free hand to her chest. "Christ Almighty, Oliver! Were you trying to scare the bejesus out of me?"

Her heart banged in her chest so violently, she was almost scared a rib was going to crack.

When she looked back up, she noticed the man was shirtless and looking perfect as ever.

Oliver moved forward again, stopping just in front of her. "Sorry, I should have made some noise so you knew I was here."

Ah, yeah. He should have. It would have saved her a near panic attack.

"That's okay." If she was honest, she was impressed with her immediate instinct to grab a weapon. Just like in the self-defense classes and at the motel, it was again confirmed that she wouldn't freeze during an attack. "How long were you standing there?"

"Not long."

Hm, why was she not sure she believed him?

Oliver put his hand out. "Can I have the knife?"

Glancing down at her hand, she realized that it was still in her grip and remained pointed right at Oliver's stomach.

"Oh. Sorry. I can put it away."

She slid the knife back in the knife block. As she did, her gaze caught on the stars outside the window. She hesitated before moving back to the sink, her eyes not leaving the twinkling lights in the sky. "I wonder if there's anyone looking at these stars right now, missing me."

Samantha maybe? Where was she? Was she safe?

Tori had this overwhelming feeling that she wasn't. Mostly, because if Samantha was safe and free, Tori was almost certain her friend would have torn down the world to find her.

Tori felt Oliver's heat on her back as he came to stand behind her. "It's possible."

Possible. Not definite.

Her hands went to the counter edge. She knew if she looked down, her knuckles would be white from how tightly she held on. But a desperation clawed at her insides. Desperation to recapture her identity. Her friend.

"I feel like I've been plunged into a dark ocean. I can't see anything. All I can hear is white noise. It's deafening." She swallowed. "I'm lost. All I want is to come up for air, but I can't find my way." Her voice cracked on the last word. She quickly swallowed. Clenched her jaw to stop from falling apart.

Oliver's hands landed on top of hers. His entire body caging her, heating her from behind. Gently, he unclenched her fingers and held them in his hands.

"You will." She felt his breath on her ear. "Even if I have to dive down there and tug you out myself."

His words had some of her desolation receding. Oliver let go of her as she turned. He didn't lift his head. His mouth was right there. "What if you drown with me?"

One hand grazed her cheek before cupping it. "No one's drowning, honey."

So certain. And strong. And confident. She needed more of that.

Lifting her hands to his shoulders, she lightly stroked his skin. "You're almost too perfect to be real."

He shook his head slowly. "I'm far from perfect."

"Me too." She barely knew herself, but she knew that. "That makes us two imperfect people. Drawn together for reasons we don't know."

His thumb stroked her cheek. "But we will. Soon."

Before she could think better of it, Tori leaned her head forward and pressed a kiss to his chest. She heard his quick intake of breath. He didn't pull away.

Why did kissing this man feel so right? Touching him...

Her hand lowered. She felt the strong pounding of his heartbeat below her palm. Tori's lips returned to his chest. Pressing more light kisses, enjoying the light rumble of his skin that came with each breath.

In the blink of an eye, she went from standing on the floor to sitting on the island. Just like earlier this evening, he wedged himself between her parted thighs. Heat cascading from her core to her limbs.

"My head's telling me this a bad idea. My heart's demanding I don't let go."

She studied his face, running a hand through his hair. "Which are you going to listen to?"

She knew which *she* wanted him to choose. Hell, she wanted to beg the man to choose his heart. Choose *her*.

She was a risk. There was no doubt about it. But she wanted him to take a chance on her.

His hands slipped under her tank top, splaying over her bare waist. "I should listen to my head..."

There was a pause. Then his mouth was on hers. Hot and demanding. No hesitation.

She tilted back as he leaned into her. Her heart soaring in her chest. The passion this man made her feel was explosive. He demanded her whole attention. Every shred of it.

Tori's legs wrapped around his waist as their mouths melded together in the most intimate way. She grabbed his shoulders, anchoring herself to him.

His hands lifted from her waist, taking hold of her top and tugging it over her head. His fingers closed around her breast.

Tori moaned deep in her throat, her head falling back. Her body throbbing. Oliver took advantage of her exposed neck, nibbling and sucking the sensitive skin.

Christ, her body was on fire. She ached for the man. Her need so intense it was almost painful.

Suddenly, the air was moving around her. Oliver walked them through the house, up the stairs, all the while keeping one hand under her and the other on her breast.

He was all power and intensity, and for tonight, he was hers. He had to be. She would surely die if he left her.

～

OLIVER LAY Tori on his bed.

He ignored the voice in his head that said this was a bad idea.

He ignored every whisper of doubt. Because she felt good. So damn good and right.

Oliver stripped off his briefs, enjoying the way her fiery eyes took in every inch of his body. Once naked, he lowered himself to the bed, removing her shorts slowly.

Fuck. The woman was magnificent. Her long brown locks fanned over the pillow. Her beautiful curves bare of any material, generous breasts completely on display.

He'd never tire of looking at her. Of exploring her soft skin with his fingers and mouth.

He kneeled at her feet, watching her with hooded eyes. "You remind me of an angel."

"Your angel," she whispered softly.

His. An unfamiliar territorial feeling pressed down on his chest. It felt both good and scary.

Lowering his head, he pressed a kiss to her ankle just above the sun that was inked to her skin. Then he moved up to her calf. Oliver trailed his mouth up the inside of her leg, stopping at the apex between her thighs.

He heard her quick intake of breath, the acceleration of her heart. Oliver lowered his head, sliding his tongue across her sensitive bundle of nerves.

Tori jolted beneath him, her hips rising off the bed.

Oliver circled her thighs with his hands, pinning her to the bed. His shoulders widened her legs farther. He swiped her in long, slow strokes. Then he paused and sucked on her clit.

The moans coming from Tori had his blood roaring in his veins. He felt himself hardening to an almost painful degree. He was vaguely aware of her fingers pulling at his hair. Her nails scraping his skin.

Removing a hand from her thigh, he inserted a finger into her, rewarded with a strangled whimper from her throat. Slowly, he pulled his finger out, before pushing back inside.

He felt every little jolt and vibration from her body as he

continued to push in and out. To suck and play with her sensitive clit.

"Oliver!" Her voice was a strangled gasp. She was close. Teetering on the edge, exactly where he wanted her.

Rising to his knees, Oliver reached across her body, opening his side drawer and grabbing a condom. Opening it, he was about to slide it over himself when Tori reached up and took it.

Slowly, she rolled the condom over his shaft. He growled softly at the feel of her touch. The pressure of her fingers.

The woman was killing him.

Leaning over her, he placed his head at her perfectly rounded breast. Taking a hard nipple into his mouth, Oliver sucked. Her nails dug into his skin. He swiped his tongue over the peak a few times. She writhed beneath him, moaning his name.

When he grazed her nipple with his teeth, she whimpered. Her fingers returned to his hair, yanking his head up. He saw the lust in her eyes. The desperation.

"I want you inside me, Oliver."

His dick twitched.

Leveraging himself on one elbow, Oliver positioned himself at her entrance, watching her features closely as he slid inside. Pleasure spread across her face as her muscles stretched to accommodate his size.

So. Damn. Perfect.

Once he was seated fully, he paused. Drinking her in. His heart did a funny kick.

Tori wrapped her legs around his waist, pulling him closer. Reaching up, she kissed him. Her lips crushing his.

Oliver lifted his hips, then pushed back inside. He just held back his groan of pleasure. It was taking every ounce of self-control not to pound into her.

The woman felt too fucking good.

He continued to thrust, loving the feel of her breasts brushing against his chest. Her feet pressed into his ass, urging him deeper.

He swallowed every moan that tried to escape her lips.

When Tori arched her back, Oliver sped up his thrusts, driving faster into her heat. Harder.

His fingers found her core and he stroked her. She tore her lips from his and threw her head back, matching his thrusts, her cries piercing the silent room.

At the sight of her so wild and lost in the throes of passion, Oliver increased his speed again. The roaring of blood in his ears so loud, it deafened him. He latched on to her neck with his mouth. Nipping her. Sucking her salty skin.

The tension built inside him. So taut, it could snap at any second.

He pinched her clit. That was it.

A strangled cry of pleasure released from her lips; she shuddered violently and came apart around him.

Oliver kept pumping, but at the feel of her walls twitching, clamping down on him, his last shred of control disappeared. Growling deep in his throat, he let his climax tear through him. Shattering him.

He held himself steady above her for long seconds, the world shifting from chaos to stillness. His breaths were long and deep. Hers short and loud.

Neither of them said a word. He didn't, *couldn't*, end the connection just yet.

Eventually, he knew he had to. Slowly, Oliver slid out of her heat, lowering himself beside her. He pulled her against his chest, wanting her close.

Tori snuggled into his side, the soft tresses of her hair splaying across his skin.

He held her as her breaths evened out. He wasn't tired. Not even close. Something had changed inside him tonight. The feelings he'd been running from, pushing aside, and trying to ignore, now slammed him right in the face as he glanced at Tori.

There was only one word to describe her. One word that felt completely unfamiliar and a bit uncomfortable in his mind.

His.

Everything he'd always believed himself to be—the lifelong bachelor, the man only focused on his mission—suddenly came into question. Tori felt right. Her living in his house, lying in his arms, felt *right*.

CHAPTER 14

*T*ori woke to a light stroke on her hip. It had traveled from the base of her back, around her hip, to just below her belly button.

Her sensitive skin heated below the waist. Lava pooling in her stomach. The breath on her neck did nothing to cool her. Neither did the rock-hard chest pressed to her back.

She almost wanted to close her eyes again, feign sleep, and enjoy the soothing comfort. But the thought of rolling over and seeing Oliver behind her was too enticing.

Tori shifted onto her back, the sheet slipping below her chest in the process. Oliver's heated gaze dropped to her breasts.

Jesus, just his gaze on her caused her stomach to do little flips. The man claimed every part of her in the most primal way.

A slow smile stretched her lips. She should probably feel shy. Shy enough to tug the sheet back up, at least. She didn't. She *couldn't*. She felt too darn happy about last night. "Good morning."

"Morning, sweetheart." His voice was honey. The hand that had just been stroking her hip shifted higher, his fingers drawing circles over her rib cage. Tori's heart pounded at the proximity of his hand to her breast. "How do you feel this morning?"

Sore and tender in the best possible way. "Good." *Great. Unbelievable.*

One of his eyebrows quirked up. "Good?"

Much better than good. But she wanted to know how he felt before she went and spilled her guts to him. "How do *you* feel?"

A shot of nerves hit her at his silence. Did he regret what they'd done?

His hand rose half an inch, stroking the underside of her breast. Her tummy dipped. Oh, sweet Jesus, that was torture. Her breast called for his attention.

"Different."

She frowned, unsure what to make of him. "Different good or bad?"

A thoughtful expression crossed his face before he smiled. "Good different."

Good different. That was a relief. He leaned in, pressing his lips to hers. At the same time, the strokes on her sensitive skin continued.

Oliver groaned. "You taste so good."

It couldn't be as good as *he* tasted.

"So you don't regret last night?" Tori blurted the question.

She only asked because yesterday, he'd walked away from her the moment his phone had rung. Almost as if he was relieved for the interruption.

"No."

There was no hesitation.

Tori wanted to be happy, but she was reluctant to trust that feeling. There were still questions. So many questions.

His lips returned to hers, his chest pressing against her bare breast. "I wish we could stay in bed longer. But Maya and Red will be here soon."

Dang it. She'd completely forgotten. They'd originally

planned a run, but because she'd rolled her ankle, they were now doing breakfast.

But then, who wouldn't forget when a man like Oliver was wreaking havoc on your body?

"How soon?" Because maybe...

"Twenty minutes."

Nope. That barely left time for a shower, let alone what she wanted.

"Guess we should get up then," she said with about as much enthusiasm as someone waiting for a tooth to be extracted.

"Hm. We should." He kissed her again, his hand rising to enclose her other breast. Oliver massaged the soft mound, causing spikes of awareness to shoot from her breast to her core.

Tori moaned deep in her throat, pushing her chest into his hand.

Too soon, the moan turned to a groan. "We need to get up." She didn't want to, but they couldn't continue. Not when Bodie could hear just as well as Oliver. He would probably hear what they were getting up to from the street. *Not* something she was overly keen for.

He pressed one last kiss to her lips before rolling away.

Tori silently cursed herself. She should have just canceled the catchup when she'd rolled her ankle. If she'd known at the time she'd be choosing between breakfast and sex, Maya would have received a speedy "next time."

Oliver stood, moving across the room completely naked and utterly flawless. He didn't have a shred of modesty. But then, who would, when they had a body like his?

Tori sat slowly, pulling the sheet to cover her chest. She studied him, wondering what had happened to the distant man from yesterday.

"How's your ankle?"

She gave it a little roll below the blanket. "Barely feel it." Just felt a bit bruised. She glanced back over to Oliver. "You can tell me, you know. If last night was a one-time thing. If you're thinking it wasn't a smart choice." It would hurt because it was the opposite of what she felt. But she would accept it. She'd have to.

He paused. He now wore shorts but no shirt. His back faced her, and she saw the slight ripple of his muscles. When he finally moved again, he grabbed a shirt from the drawer before turning to face her.

"I would tell you if that was how I felt." He pulled the shirt on before moving toward her. His mouth hovered over hers, his breath fanning her face. "Last night was amazing, honey." He kissed her, long and slow, before lifting his head. "I'll make some coffee before they arrive."

Then he was gone.

Amazing.

Gah. Tori fell back into bed again, unable to wipe the huge smile from her lips.

Eventually, she climbed out of bed. The first couple steps she went slow on her ankle, but quickly realized she didn't even need to limp.

Grabbing one of his shirts from the drawer, she tugged it over her head before moving to the room she'd been staying in.

Last night had been so much more than she'd expected. She'd *felt* so much more than she'd expected. Protected. Safe. Happy...

Had she felt all that the first time they'd been together?

Tori had a quick shower before pulling on a pair of shorts and T-shirt. When she headed downstairs, the first thing she saw was Oliver placing two coffees on the kitchen island.

He was smiling. The hooded expression she'd been greeted with previous mornings nowhere to be seen. "I made us a quick coffee."

Oliver handed her the drink, his fingers grazing hers in the process. A zing of electricity ran up her arm. She took a small sip before placing it back down on the island. "Sorry, but…is it okay if I grab a juice?"

He tilted his head. "Not a fan of my coffee-making skills?"

She chuckled. "Your coffee-making skills are great. I've just never been a huge fan of coffee."

Oliver had made it here and there since she'd moved in with him, but this morning, especially after their night together, she could use the sugar hit of some juice.

"Quinn would have a fit if she heard that." He chuckled. "Of course."

Oliver started to set his coffee on the island but Tori shook her head, already moving toward the fridge. "I'll get it."

Pulling the fridge door open, she grabbed the orange juice before getting a glass from the cabinet. She'd only just begun pouring when a memory flashed through her mind.

Tori poured the wine halfway up the glass before shooting a glance over her shoulder. He was still clearing the table. His back turned.

With trembling fingers, she yanked the capsule from her pocket, twisting it open and pouring the powder in.

Her heart hammered in her chest.

The bottle of orange juice slammed to the counter hard as Tori returned to the present. Quick breaths whooshed in and out of her chest.

What the hell had she just remembered?

"Tori?"

She jolted at Oliver's voice. Slowly, she turned to face him.

Tori turned to face Oliver, glasses of wine in hand. Oliver walked toward her. He had that same sexy smile stretching his lips.

Her stomach convulsed as a sick feeling hit her hard and fast.

It didn't feel right. It hadn't been feeling right all day. He couldn't be the man they told her he was. She'd only spent a day with him, yet she knew. He just couldn't be.

He reached for the glass closest to him. The one she'd dosed.

Sucking in a sharp breath, Tori took a hurried step back, hitting the counter with her hip. The glass dropped from her fingers.

She knew he'd reach for it. Knew the speed he possessed.

Before he could, Tori spun toward the glass, making it appear like she was trying to catch it, when in reality, she was blocking it from his reach.

Warm hands grasped Tori's shoulders, giving her a gentle shake.

Her eyes flew to Oliver's worried ones. Her world screeching to a halt.

She'd almost drugged him. She didn't know what the powder was, but it couldn't have been anything good.

Suddenly, an overwhelming urge to throw up hit her system. Tears pricked the back of her eyes.

"Tori. Did you remember something?" Alarm coated his voice. "What did you see?"

She opened and shut her lips. No words came out. She had no words to give. What could she say? *Sorry, I'm not the good guy we were both hoping?*

Oh god, how would he ever forgive her? *She* couldn't forgive her.

Swallowing the nausea, Tori yanked herself from his hold and turned around. She'd taken two steps away when he was there, in front of her, looking big and powerful. He stood between the island and the counter, boxing her in.

"Tori...talk to me." There was a new edge to his voice. A hardness that hadn't been there moments ago. He knew whatever she'd seen, it wasn't good.

She shook her head, willing her voice to work. "I didn't see anything."

It was a weak lie. Which was fitting, considering how damn weak her entire body felt.

His eyes narrowed. He was looking less and less like the

protector she'd woken up with and more like a predator. "You're lying. Tell me the truth."

The truth...

That they hadn't met by accident. That she'd sought him out to hurt him. Almost drugged him.

She took a hurried step back, and quick as lightning, Oliver's arm shot out and took hold of her arm. His touch was gentle, but it was also firm. Unyielding. A manacle holding her in place.

Oliver stepped forward, a steeliness in his gaze. The man looked every bit as deadly as he was. "Tori. If the memory involves me or my brothers, we need to know."

Then his features softened a fraction. His fingers grazed her cheek.

Her heart broke a little bit in her chest. He would hate her. How could he not?

Tori swallowed. She took a breath, not sure if a truth or lie was about to come out—but a knock on the door interrupted her. Her mouth snapped shut.

Oliver growled low in his throat. "Come back another time."

Tori shook her head. No. He would force it out of her. She wasn't ready for that.

"Stay." She barely spoke above a whisper. "Please."

The panic in her chest was suffocating her. Panic of losing him. Again. She'd had him for less than a day and already she couldn't let go.

A moment of silence passed. Tori wondered if the person who'd knocked had walked away. Then the click of the door unlocking sounded.

Relief was instant as Bodie stepped inside. He took in the scene in front of him. "Ah, hope you don't mind. I used the spare key."

Because he'd heard the desperation in her voice? Or maybe because he'd heard the fear.

Maya stepped in behind him, looking far more at ease, not having heard what Bodie had.

She smiled at Tori. "Hey! Ready to go? We ran here and I'm starving."

To Maya, it probably looked like she and Oliver were in an intimate embrace. Oliver holding her arm. Standing close enough to kiss her.

Tori forced a smile to her lips. It probably looked wonky and all kinds of wrong. "Yep. Let's go."

Summoning her courage, Tori looked back to Oliver. His mouth was set in a thin line. His jaw hard.

Anger. And frustration.

His fingers didn't loosen. Would he cause a scene in front of his friends? Would he force words from her that she'd rather cut off her own hand than speak right now?

Three seconds passed. Finally, his hand dropped. He stepped back. But the man never took his eyes off her. Not for a second. He continued to stare at her as if he knew what *she* knew.

As if she'd already exposed her true nature.

CHAPTER 15

*O*liver watched Tori from a few feet away. They stood inside Joan's Diner, waiting for food to takeaway and planned to eat outside. She was laughing lightly at something Maya said. Oliver saw right through it. Strain lines edged her eyes. Her jaw was tense, like she was using all her energy to hold her smile in place.

What had she seen? What memory had she recovered that was so terrible, she couldn't share it? The way her skin had gone a pasty white told him it couldn't be good.

He needed to know, dammit. But the woman had looked like she was going to be sick. Either that or pass out.

Oliver could have forced it. Hell, he'd interrogated some of the meanest criminals in the world. But there was no way he was about to use any of those tactics on her.

Bodie stepped away from the register to stand beside Oliver. He kept his gaze diverted as he spoke, his voice low. "So what's going on? Why did Tori look like she needed saving back there?"

There was accusation in Bodie's voice. And Oliver knew why. Tori had sounded scared. His heart clenched. He didn't want her scared of him. He just wanted the truth. "She remembered something."

Bodie was silent for a moment. "And?"

"And she wouldn't tell me what. But it was bad. You should have seen the way the color drained from her face."

Bodie finally looked at him. "How did you react when she wouldn't tell you?"

Oliver ran a hand through his hair. "I just asked her to tell me what she remembered." Then had gotten frustrated when she wouldn't.

"If you want to find out, I think you'll need to make her feel comfortable enough to share."

Bodie was right. Of course he was. But... "What if I don't like what she tells me?"

What they'd shared last night had changed something in him. He finally felt like he could let someone in. Have a relationship. But if she wasn't who he'd hoped, that wouldn't just put Oliver's life in danger, it would endanger the entire team.

"I get what you're saying." Bodie nodded. "This is important. Whatever she's hiding, it involves Carter and Hylar. That means it involves us."

Exactly. It wasn't just about Oliver. He had to think about his brothers. He didn't have much choice. "I need to know. And I need to know soon."

"One of us can question her if it's easier."

Oliver was already shaking his head. "It needs to be me."

TORI WET HER LIPS. She felt Oliver's eyes on her. Searching. Demanding. She wanted to squirm, but Maya was still talking and she needing to fake it. Fake that she was okay. That the man she was falling for wasn't about to find out her ugly truth.

Maya paused mid-sentence, a frown creasing her brows. "Tori, are you okay?"

She wasn't faking it so well, was she? Even Maya could see her struggle. "Of course."

The other woman studied Tori's eyes, concern flickering through her own. "Let's go to the bathroom."

Tori didn't have a chance to respond before Maya was taking hold of her hand and tugging her toward the back of the diner. She called something out to Bodie over her shoulder before stepping into the hall.

Instead of going to the women's bathroom, Maya pulled them into the disabled one, locking the door with a resounding click.

Maya stepped close. "Now, are you okay?"

Her soft voice, in combination with her empathetic eyes, caused some of the pain Tori had been holding in, shielding from the world, to leak out. For the second time that day, tears burned the back of her eyes. Emotion clogging her throat. "I saw something this morning. A memory."

And I'm struggling to accept it as reality.

"It must have been bad to put that look on your face. Whatever it was, it'll be okay."

Tori wasn't so sure. "I don't think it will. I like Oliver. A lot." One night together and everything felt different. "I'm so scared."

She knew she wasn't making sense. Her words were jumbled. Just like her mind.

The concern on Maya's face shifted to confusion. "What are you scared of?"

"That I'm part of the evil that Oliver and his team are hunting."

Saying those words out loud made them so much more real.

She swallowed a sob, not wanting to fall apart. Not here. Tori looked down at her hands, not able to meet the other woman's gaze. "I think maybe that weekend we met, I was supposed to do something bad to Oliver. I didn't,"—*couldn't*—"but that was my intention."

Her mission.

The idea of telling Oliver made her want to run away. Hide somewhere she'd never be found, where the truth would never be known.

Maya touched her arm. "Tori, we haven't known each other long...but I don't think you're a bad person. And if you were meant to do something terrible to Oliver, but didn't, that's proof right there."

It was proof that he'd affected her on a deep level. That she'd felt enough for him to not want to hurt him. It wasn't proof that she was a good person.

"We don't know *who* I am, Maya. Where I live, who my family is. We don't even know if Tori is my real name!" Panic began to bubble inside her. "Who the hell am I?"

Her voice broke on the last word. Had she come to Marble Falls specifically to hurt Oliver? Even to *kill* him?

Just as Tori was whirling into a full-blown panic attack, Maya pulled her into her arms. The other woman held her so tightly, it felt like her arms were the only thing keeping Tori together.

"You're Tori." Maya spoke quietly into her ear. "The woman who came to Marble Falls looking for answers. The woman who found Oliver and connected with him. Who is genuinely concerned for his wellbeing." She released her, looking her dead in the eye. "From what I've seen, you're determined, kind, and strong. You don't need memories to know who you are. It's in here." Maya placed a hand above Tori's heart.

She wanted to believe her. But she couldn't deny that memory. "I don't want him to hate me." *To look at me like I'm his enemy.*

"Tell him what you remembered this morning. Trust him with your truth. When I made the decision to trust Bodie with mine, everything became easier."

Trust Oliver. It sounded easy. But her truth was probably a bit different from Maya's.

She shook her head, forcing a smile she didn't feel to her lips. "We should get back out there, our food's probably ready. Thank you."

"Are you okay?"

No. "Yes."

Maya gave Tori another hug before leading them back out toward the front of the diner. Oliver was still standing beside Bodie, looking beautiful and dangerous. She risked a quick peek at his face. His gaze was intense and entirely focused on her.

Her eyes darted away.

Bodie lifted the bag in his hand. "Got the food. We gonna eat at the park?"

Tori noticed that Oliver held a bag in his hand too.

Maya threaded her fingers through Bodie's other hand. "We're going to jog home. Oliver and Tori are going to take the car and have breakfast at their house. They have stuff they need to talk about."

The thought of being alone with Oliver had her skin prickling. Not because she thought he'd hurt her. Because she didn't know how she was going to voice what needed to be said.

Bodie nodded, looking like he understood what she was saying. "Sounds good."

It didn't take nearly long enough to say their goodbyes. To climb into Oliver's car and drive back to his home.

The closer they drew to his house, the more her gut clenched. By the time Oliver closed the front door, all her fine hairs were standing on end.

He placed the food on the kitchen island before turning toward her. He looked a foot taller than he had yesterday. Broader. Stronger.

Nope. She couldn't do it.

"I'm going to have a shower."

She'd barely made it two steps before he was in front of her. Blocking her exit once again. "You've had some time to digest what you saw. Now I need to know, Tori."

Time to digest? She didn't feel like she'd digested anything. She'd rebelled against it. "You don't want to eat first?"

"Tori..."

She was out of time.

He took a step closer. When his hand reached to touch her, she gave a small flinch.

The frown on Oliver's face told her he'd noticed. He looked worried. "Please."

She swallowed. "I don't want to tell you."

The frown on his face deepened. "Why?"

"Because I'm scared you're going to hate me."

He shook his head. "I won't."

But he could...probably would.

She didn't draw her eyes away from his. Instead, she took a breath and said the words that could destroy them. "That glass of wine that I poured you that night...the one I dropped..." *Oh god, just say it, Tori. There's no way to soften the blow.* "I took a capsule out of my pocket and emptied the contents into the glass. Your glass."

The last part probably wasn't necessary. But she said it anyway. To bring home the point of what happened. That she'd almost drugged him.

He was still. So still, she wondered if he was breathing. His expression didn't change.

"Oliver—"

"Did you drop the glass on purpose?"

The one small reprieve of this terrible admission. "Yes." Did that make her redeemable?

He studied her face, no doubt looking for any signs of deceit. "Do you remember why you made the decision to drop it?"

"I remember thinking that you weren't the man they told me you were."

Oliver nodded slowly. His blank expression still giving nothing away. "So they told you I was someone I wasn't, then sent you here, with instructions to drug me. When you chose not to, they tried to kill you."

"That's the most likely narrative."

The next logical question was, why had she been willing to drug him in the first place? He didn't ask that question. Knew she didn't know the answer yet.

He took a step back. She felt the distance immediately.

"Thank you for telling me. I need to tell my team."

Oliver walked away...and every step he took had Tori feeling more alone. More like the bad guy she'd started to suspect she was.

Tori hadn't drugged the man, but she'd still hurt him. She'd highlighted how vulnerable he'd made himself by letting her get too close. She'd walked into this town, into his home, earned the man's trust, then smashed it to pieces.

CHAPTER 16

*T*he knock on Tori's door had a smile pulling at her lips. She knew it was Samantha. Her friend had messaged to say she was five minutes away. That had been about fifteen minutes ago.

"It's unlocked."

Even if it wasn't, Samantha had a key. The woman was probably just trying to get Tori off the couch. A place she'd found herself way too often lately.

The door burst open and Samantha entered. She was like a ray of sunlight with her bright blond curls and beaming smile. It was one of the things Tori loved about her.

Samantha dropped onto the couch beside Tori. "Care to share why my three texts went unanswered today."

Tori scoffed. "Three? Try ten."

"Uh-huh! You did see them."

Of course she had. Every one of them.

Reaching beside her, Tori lifted her tea. Her now cold tea. "Yes. I did. I didn't think pictures of cats wearing shark costumes required responses."

Samantha sighed. "You disappoint me, my friend. Those hilarious *images that I scoured the Internet for and individually selected for your entertainment definitely deserved a response."*

The pictures had made Tori smile. Something she hadn't been doing a whole lot of during her empty days. She wouldn't be telling Samantha that though. The woman would send another twenty tomorrow.

"I'm more of a dog person." Tori reached over and patted Charlie. He was always close by. Just the way she liked it.

"Well, at least you didn't try to tell me you've been busy. We all know watching Friends *reruns does not qualify as busy."* Samantha took the tea from her fingers, taking a sip before Tori could warn her. Samantha spluttering half of it back out. *"What the heck? This is stone-cold."*

Tori tried to hide her chuckle. *"I wouldn't say stone-cold. Definitely not hot though."*

It was also the third cup of tea she'd let go cold that day. Another fun fact she wouldn't be sharing with her friend.

Samantha placed the cup on the coffee table. *"That's it. This needs to stop right now."*

"What needs to stop?" Her daytime TV watching or drinking cold tea?

"All of it," Samantha said, basically reading Tori's mind. *"Lucky for your unemployed butt, my boss needs someone to complete a job for him. He mentioned it to me, and I suggested you."*

That had Tori's lethargic brain shooting to alert. *"Your boss has a job that you suggested me for?"*

"Yep."

Tori straightened, not sure she was hearing her friend properly. *"Samantha, you're a biomedical engineer. You work for some government department doing military research. Your current project is so secret, you can't even tell me what you're doing."*

"That's correct."

"What could your boss possibly want with an unemployed Army dropout."

A small frown marred Samantha's brow. "You're not an Army dropout. You served your two terms, now you're having a break."

Yeah. But at what point did a "break" just become "unemployed"?

"What's the job?"

"He mentioned he needs someone—a woman—to bring in a target. Some guy who's a threat to the military."

"Sammy, I'm not a cop."

"He knows who you are. The department did crazy-thorough checks on everyone in my life when I got the job."

Yeah, Samantha had mentioned that a few times, and Tori still didn't love it. Still, this request was completely different from anything she'd done in the military. "Why did you suggest me?"

"Because you're a woman. You know how to defend yourself. And you need a new direction. This could be it."

She nibbled her lip. "Wouldn't someone in his position have the ability to choose the best in the business for something like this?"

Samantha lifted a shoulder. "Maybe after I told him you could do it, he stopped looking. He wants someone skilled in subterfuge. Someone who knows how to tell the truth without giving away any actual information, especially personal."

Giving away nothing personal would be easy. What would she say? That she was bored? Grieving? Had absolutely no desire to live the life that she used to live?

"And he knows I'm all these things because he's done a background check on me too?"

"Tori, this project I'm working on is massive. It will change everything. They have to do their due diligence and make sure me and the people around me are trustworthy."

Didn't change her opinion on the matter of privacy.

"Just come talk to Hylar. This job is right up your alley. You love taking down bad guys. It's why you joined the Army." She covered Tori's hand with her own. "Plus, I'm worried about you."

Oh god. Tori had been waiting for this. She knew it was only a matter of time before she got "the chat" from her friend.

"It's been six months since your mom passed away."

Tori tried unsuccessfully not to flinch at Samantha's words. She would never get used to the reality of her mom being gone.

She swallowed. "I know how long it's been, Sammy. Just like I know it's been almost two years since yours passed away."

Samantha didn't flinch at all. She'd always been stronger than Tori.

"I've had more time to come to terms with it than you."

Was it possible to come to terms with the death of a parent? Both Tori and Samantha were born into single-parent households. Neither had a father around to soften the blow.

"When we met in the oncology ward at the hospital, I knew we'd become best friends. You're the badass to my geek. So I'm entitled to be worried about you."

And Tori had been unbelievably grateful to have met Samantha ever since. The one good thing to come out of that place. "I'm okay, Samantha. It's been hard," unbelievably hard, "but I'm surviving."

"I know. And I want to help you in any way I can."

"And getting me a job taking down some big bad criminal is you helping me?"

Some of Samantha's spunk came back. "Hell yes, it is. I want to see your badass side come out again."

Tori frowned. "What's wrong with my sitting-on-the-couch-drink-ing-cold-tea side?"

Samantha wrinkled her nose. "Let's not go into that right now." She reached for the remote. "I'm glad we've decided you're taking the job. Maybe this will turn into something long term for you." Samantha flicked to the Netflix main page.

"Hey! I was watching that."

"And now you're not." Her friend popped her feet onto the coffee table, the half sun tattoo on her right ankle poking out from below her pant leg.

Tori shook her head. "Fine. But no science documentaries, okay?"

"Boo, you're no fun."

Tori's eyes popped open. For a moment, she just lay there.

Taking in the dream. The memory. Her mind working overtime to analyze everything she'd just learned.

Samantha worked for Hylar. That's how Tori had become entangled in all this. Had her friend realized who she was working for?

Tori shook her head. No. Over the last few days, memories had slipped into her consciousness. Memories of Samantha. Of their friendship. Tori may not remember everything about her friend, but she knew enough.

Samantha wouldn't have put Tori in danger. Not intentionally.

Climbing out of bed, Tori walked over to the window. She pushed back the curtain and looked up at the moon and stars.

Where are you, Samantha? Are you searching for me? Are you worried? Or are you as lost as I am?

God, she hoped her friend was safe. But she worked for Hylar —the man Oliver called his enemy. Chances were slim.

As she watched the stars, she let the other part of her dream wash over her.

Her mother was dead.

Tori's heart seized in pain. She couldn't remember her mom. She couldn't even tell someone what color the woman's eyes were. But Tori still felt the weight of the loss.

A tear slipped down her cheek. If there was a time she needed a best friend or a mother, it was now.

A feeling of complete loneliness hit her like a ton of bricks. For the last week, Oliver had been friendly but distant. She was living in his house but not sleeping in his bed. She felt like an unwelcome guest. Like someone he was keeping a close eye on, rather than someone he was trying to help and protect.

She'd considered leaving more than once. But it was impossible. The man was always there. Watching. Listening. He hadn't said she had to stay, but she felt it all the same. He needed to know her truth as much as she did.

There was also the small part of her that didn't want to leave. That was choosing the company of a man who saw her as a threat over the loneliness of being out in the world on her own.

Another tear fell.

Oliver had probably woken at the sound of her climbing out of bed, but he wouldn't come in. She'd gotten up to watch the stars almost every night. The man never checked on her.

At least now she knew. She'd almost drugged Oliver because they'd told her he was a threat. She'd thought she was completing a job for a government agency.

Oliver wasn't a threat. And they weren't the government.

Would he want her again if she told him about her latest memory? Would she earn back some of his trust?

No. Oliver had made it clear this last week that he didn't want her any longer. That their one night together had been a momentary lapse in judgment.

More tears fell. Tears for the loss of her mother. Tears for the loss of her best friend. And tears for the fact that she'd fallen for a man who didn't feel the same way.

CHAPTER 17

Oliver took a sip of his coffee. He was running today's women's self-defense class with Bodie, and he had fifteen minutes before it was due to start.

Christ, he was glad Marble Protection had a commercial-grade coffee machine. He didn't want to think about how much he'd slept over the last week. It wasn't nearly enough.

Fortunately, his body didn't need much, but so many consecutive shit nights were starting to catch up with him.

The door to the kitchen opened and Kye walked in. "You look like hell."

Guess he looked how he felt then. "Thanks."

Kye folded his arms, leaning his hip on the kitchen counter. "Okay, give it to me straight. What's going on? Ever since Tori told you about the wine incident, you've been walking around this place like someone stabbed you in the thigh then ran over your cat."

A stab wound to his thigh would probably have been less painful. "I'm fine. I've called a briefing with the team after my class to go over Tori's most recent memory."

Tori had told him about her dream that morning. About her

being in the Army. Thinking she was working for a government organization.

She wasn't an enemy. She'd been duped.

"Good. I look forward to hearing about it. Now tell me about you."

Clearly, "fine" had not cut it. But he didn't feel like talking about himself, dammit.

Oliver studied his friend. Noting his set features and unyielding stance. The guy wasn't going to let this go. He scrubbed a hand over his face. "I'm angry."

"At yourself?"

"Yes. I almost allowed a woman I'd just met to drug me. A woman connected to Hylar. Imagine for a second that she had. That she'd given me that drink with whatever the hell it contained. I would have either been killed or taken."

The muscles in Kye's arms visibly tensed. "Would have been hell for everyone. I don't think Hylar would have killed you though. I think he would have taken you. And we would have found you."

So much damn confidence in his friend's voice. "There's no guarantee that you would have found me. And who knows what you would have had to do to get me back."

"Whatever was necessary."

Exactly. His team would have put themselves in the line of danger for him. After he'd been stupid enough to put himself in a compromised position to begin with.

Kye took a step forward. "You weren't taken though. Tori didn't give you the drug. You're here. She's here. And she's trying to help in whatever way she can."

He knew all that. Didn't ease his frustration.

"What's going on between you and Tori?"

"Nothing."

He wasn't even lying. He'd barely spoken to the woman all week. Because he knew that if he did, he'd want her again.

Then this morning's revelation. Suddenly, she wasn't the bad guy. He *could* have her. And he wanted her, dammit. But something was stopping him.

One of Kye's brows lifted. "Because you're pushing her away?"

"I can't get over the fact that I made myself so vulnerable."

That wasn't Tori's fault. It was entirely his.

Kye placed his hands on Oliver's shoulders. "Forgive yourself."

Easier said than done.

Kye sighed. "This new memory, the reason for today's meeting...is it bad?"

"She was in the Army, so I'm going to get Wyatt to try and find her record." He paused before adding the next part. "Also, her best friend, Samantha, was a biomedical engineer. She worked for Hylar, thinking she was working for a government department."

Kye's body went unnaturally still. "Biomedical engineer?"

Yeah, Kye was thinking the same thing Oliver was. That *anything* combining engineering principles with medicine and science should not be connected to Hylar. It was a recipe for disaster.

"That's how Tori got pulled into this," Oliver continued. "I was a job that Hylar asked her to complete."

Kye stood silent. A crease between his brows.

Oliver set his coffee on the counter. "I slept with someone connected to our enemy without realizing it. Gave her access to my home. Let her get close enough to hurt me. It just makes me think that maybe Hylar's been right all along. Maybe letting people in, creating relationships and connections, is a weakness."

~

"Is he still avoiding you?" Maya asked.

Tori bent over and touched her toes, feeling the stretch run through her calf muscles. "He's barely spoken two words to me. The man has calm and distant down pat."

He could be the king of the damn club.

Maya pulled her right arm across her body, stretching her shoulder muscles. "He probably just needs time."

Tori had told Maya about each new memory she'd regained. Maya's friendship had become something she relied on. Especially now, since she was the only person Tori could talk to.

"Maybe." Or maybe Oliver's just waiting for her to regain her full memory so he could have all the information before sending her away.

Tori straightened as Oliver and Bodie entered the space and went to stand in front of the class.

At least now she knew where she'd learned to fight. It wasn't some underground fighting ring or through some sort of gang activity. She'd been in the Army. One small comfort.

The women in the room quieted as Bodie began explaining today's lesson—striking the attacker with the palm. Bodie grabbed one of the rubber mannequins from the side of the room and placed it in front of Oliver.

Oliver demonstrated the correct striking technique. Even though he looked like he put very little behind the hit, the mannequin's head flew backward, evidence of the strength Oliver possessed.

Tori hadn't seen Oliver fight before, but he looked like he'd be deadly. The man was all power.

When the demonstration was complete, one woman from each pair grabbed a mannequin.

Maya went first. Her strikes were light and a tad uncoordinated. Bodie walked over, positioned himself behind her and guided her hits. They'd already explained that it wasn't just the strike itself that was important. It was the footwork and body positioning too. That's where the power came from.

When it was Tori's turn, she positioned herself in front of the mannequin, shuffled her feet and hit it with her palm—hard. Just like with every other self-defense activity, this one felt familiar. Her body remembered what to do.

She positioned herself again. *Foot shuffle, palm strike.* She repeated the sequence a few times.

When she saw Oliver heading her way, she tried to ignore the quick acceleration of her heart rate. A week ago, and her heart would have been pounding in excitement at the sight of him coming toward her. Today, she felt more dread than anything else.

Just like Bodie had to Maya, Oliver stood behind her, turning her body. "You need to be more side on."

Tori sucked in a deep breath at the feel of his gentle but firm hands on her waist. It was the first time he'd touched her in a week. She felt it everywhere.

Oliver dropped his hands and stepped away.

Foot shuffle, palm strike.

Then his hands were back on her. Twisted her body farther to the side.

Tori attempted the sequence three more times. After each one, Oliver found something to correct.

Finally, she blew out a frustrated breath, dropping her hands. "I don't need your corrections. I know what I'm doing." She knew because her movements came to her instinctively.

Oliver's gaze narrowed. "Okay." He held his hands up in front of him. "Go."

She frowned. "You want me to strike your hands?" The man wasn't even wearing protection.

"Yes. And I want you to put a hell of a lot more power into it than what you were just using."

Irritation washed over Tori. A muscle ticked in her jaw. If he was trying to annoy her, he was succeeding. She positioned herself in front of him.

Foot shuffle, palm strike.

She paused, expecting to see him in some sort of pain. She hadn't hit him lightly.

He was completely fine. "Again."

Tori repeated the sequence. Then again. On each hit, Oliver let his hand stretch back a fraction, easing the pressure on her wrist.

He nodded. "Now harder."

She did as he asked. Striking harder. Throwing more force into it.

It was ten more hits before he nodded, dropping his hands. "Good. Let's add a left hook punch at the end."

He wanted her to *punch* his hand? Still with no protection?

When he held his hands up, Tori quieted the questions in her head. If that was what he wanted, then that's what he'd get.

Shuffle, palm strike, punch.

Again, his hands gave way slightly on each contact, easing the impact.

Her breathing started to become labored, but Tori didn't stop.

"Harder, Tori. If you need to hit someone to survive, this isn't gonna cut it."

She repeated the sequence again, harder. Ignoring her aching shoulders. "You mean if I need to survive someone like *you*." The words were spoken quietly enough that they only reached his ears.

"Yes. Someone like me. But *not* me."

Shuffle, palm strike, punch.

"You never know. I might need to protect myself against you." Her breathing was so labored, she only just got the words out.

The frustration and anger of the last week—hell, the last month—welled in her chest.

"Why would you need to protect yourself against me?"

She almost wanted to laugh at his question. Either that or cry. "For the same reason you've been keeping me at a distance." *Shuf-*

fle, palm strike, punch. "I might pose a threat to you and your friends. You might need to eliminate me."

She'd told him about her last memory, hoping he would finally trust her again. He'd given her no sign that anything had changed.

When Oliver didn't reply, Tori snuck a look in between hits. His brows were drawn together. "Do you think you pose a threat to me or my friends?"

"Does it matter what I think? If *you* think I'm a threat, maybe I am."

She didn't think she was a threat. And her dream last night had confirmed it. She was just tired, and a week of being ignored was starting to wear on her.

"I don't think you're a threat, Tori." Could have fooled her. "Is there anything you haven't told me?"

Shuffle, palm strike, punch. "Yes." She was breathing heavily now. "My mother died seven months ago. Cancer. And I feel like I've lost her all over again."

Oliver's hands dropped. Tori didn't realize in time, throwing the last punch and hitting him in the shoulder. His shoulder didn't give way like his hands had. It was like hitting a brick wall.

Tori squeaked at the sudden sharp pang to her wrist. Grabbing her wrist, she bent over. Breathing through the pain.

"Dammit." She felt the heat of Oliver as he moved to her side. "Are you okay?"

She nodded, tears prickling her eyes.

One of Oliver's arms slid around her waist and the other wrapped behind her legs. Then he swept her off her feet and headed toward the hall. He continued to curse to himself, his body stiff with tension around her.

When they reached the office, he placed her gently on the couch and crouched in front of her. He pulled out his phone. "Sage, are you free? Tori hurt her wrist and may need an x-ray."

Tori shook her head. "I don't need an x-ray. I'm fine."

"Yes, we can be at the hospital in ten minutes."

Was the man ignoring her? *"You* may be there in ten minutes. I won't."

"Sage, hang on." He lowered the phone from his ear. "Tori, you need an x-ray."

"I don't. It doesn't hurt enough to be a fracture or break."

His eyes narrowed. "It's safer to get it checked."

"No."

Oliver looked about ready to blow up. "Sage, are you able to come here and look at it first? Not sure if you can tell us if an x-ray is needed by doing a physical exam...?" There was a brief pause. "See you soon." Hanging up, he shoved his phone back into his pocket.

"I can wait here for Sage while you finish the class." The lesson wasn't even halfway done.

Oliver shook his head. "Kye and Eden are around somewhere. Bodie will grab one of them." Oliver looked like he was going to say something else, then seemed to change his mind. "I'm gonna grab some ice."

Once he stepped out of the room, Tori studied her wrist. It was slightly swollen and only hurt when she moved it.

Oliver didn't take long. When he returned, he crouched to his haunches in front of her again and pressed an ice pack wrapped in a towel around her wrist.

She expected him to drop her arm. He didn't. He continued to hold it. The heat of his body radiating off him into her.

"Sage said it will likely need an x-ray but she's willing to look at it first."

Tori nodded. If a doctor told her she needed one, there really wasn't much she could do.

"Tell me about your mom."

Tori stiffened, his soft words catching her off guard. One of his hands shifted to her leg, closing around her thigh just above the knee.

"There's not much to tell. Samantha and I met in the hospital when both our mothers had cancer. Her mother passed away a couple of years ago and my mom died seven months ago." Tori swallowed the lump in her throat. "Today, I've been remembering bits and pieces about her. Her smile. Her voice. It sounds crazy to be grieving her loss when I barely remember her."

Oliver's hand tightened a fraction. "You don't need to remember everything, to remember that you loved and lost."

She swallowed again. "I remember how important she was to me. The hole in my life once she was gone." She cast her eyes down, wanting to hide the pain she knew was all over her face.

She felt Oliver's forehead touch hers. "I'm sorry." His words were whispered, but they could have been shouted, she heard them so clearly.

Tori blinked back her tears. "Thank you."

Oliver touched his finger to her chin, tilting her head up. When she met his gaze, she saw both empathy and regret. "I wish you'd come to me last night. I know why you didn't…but I wish you had."

She nodded, then looked away. She wished she had too.

CHAPTER 18

Oliver watched Tori from the corner of his eyes as he made grilled cheese sandwiches.

She was sitting on the couch, picking at the wrapping on her wrist. It had only been bandaged for a day and he could tell she was already getting frustrated by it.

He clenched his jaw as he placed the cheese on the bread. Her injury was his fault, and he hated that. He'd been distracted for a second. That was all it took.

Sage had been able to tell from the physical exam that it was just a strain. Lots of icing and rest were required. Didn't help ease his guilt. The woman had already rolled her ankle and fallen into a river, and now this. He was doing a bang-up job of protecting her.

Shaking his head, he placed the sandwiches on the griddle.

He'd tried to distance himself from her. He'd spent a week torturing himself by doing just that. But yesterday, seeing the pain she'd tried to hide creeping into her eyes, the desolation, it damn near tore his heart in two.

Tori had thought she was working for a government agency. She hadn't intentionally worked for the wrong side. And Kye was right, Oliver needed to quit beating himself up about letting a woman he barely knew get close to him.

He shot a quick look at his watch. Kye would be here in five minutes to watch Tori while he trained. He *needed* to train. To blow off some steam. Exert his body. Exhaust himself. Even though it was damn near impossible.

He pulled the sandwiches off the griddle, plated them, and brought one to Tori.

"Thanks." She lifted the plate. "I swear, the smell of grilled cheese is the most delicious smell in the world. I was drooling while it was cooking."

Drooling should be a turnoff. When Tori said it, it wasn't. Jeez, he was screwed.

"Grilled cheese is a favorite of mine, too. Although not sure I would go so far as labeling it the most delicious smell in the world."

If they were talking anything, non-specific to food, then there was definitely a certain woman whose scent drove him crazy. She had more of a cinnamon and strawberry kind of smell to her.

"How's your wrist feeling today?"

Tori lifted a shoulder. "I barely feel it. The bandaging is more itchy than anything. Sage did say it was pretty mild." She looked at him, sandwich halfway to her mouth. "You're not beating yourself up about it, are you?"

Yeah, he definitely was. "I should have protected you from the injury."

Her eyes softened. "I'm okay. It's more annoying than anything."

Oliver nodded. It still shouldn't have happened. Not under his watch. "Have you remembered anything about Hylar?"

And just like that, the light in her eyes dimmed. "No."

Footsteps sounded outside seconds before Kye walked in. "I can smell that grilled cheese from the street. Tell me you made your best bud one."

Tori chuckled. "I tried to tell him it was the best smell in the world."

Oliver pointed to the kitchen. "Yours is on the island."

Kye's smile broadened. "You know me too well."

You didn't need to know Kye that well to know the man had an appetite.

Kye took a seat on the other side of the couch. "How we holding up today? Any more injuries to add to the ankle and wrist? Did you try headbutting his hard head today?"

Oliver mumbled under his breath while Tori chuckled again. Her laugh was lyrical. Like a damn bird song.

"Not yet," Tori said in between bites. "But the day's still young, give it time."

"There won't be any more injuries," Oliver growled.

Tori nodded. "Yeah, let's hope he doesn't make me want to hit him. It's like punching a brick wall."

Kye shook his head. "Wish people knew *I* was built like a brick wall. Would save them a lot of broken bones."

Tori grinned. "You get punched a lot?"

Oliver scoffed. "Not nearly enough." A cushion hurled his way. Oliver caught to easily. "The guy likes to rile people up. They get mad."

"That's why I don't widen my circle of friends." Kye put his already empty plate on the table. "These guys have a good lid on their temper. Well, except for Hunter. I don't piss that guy off."

The small frown that creased Tori's brow was cute. "Hunter. And you're Cage." She turned to Oliver. "Why do they call you Ax?"

"My middle name is Axel. Oliver Axel Bolten. The guys thought Oliver was too long and didn't shorten well."

Kye laughed. "We're a lazy bunch, us military guys."

Tori paused, seeming to mull something over in her head. "Maybe..." She stopped.

"What is it?"

"Maybe my middle name is Tori."

Oliver shot a look to Kye and then back to Tori. "You don't think Tori's your first name?"

She lifted a shoulder. "I don't know. It doesn't sound all that familiar for me to introduce myself as Tori. And no one has been able to locate a Tori near where I was found."

They'd assumed that if her name wasn't Tori, she would have remembered by now. But maybe not.

"Did Carter or your friend Samantha call you Tori in your dreams?" Kye asked, voicing the very question Oliver was about to ask.

Tori's face dropped. "Yeah. Samantha did."

Not promising. But still... "It's a good thought. We can look into it."

One side of her mouth lifted.

Oliver stood, taking his and Kye's plates to the kitchen. "I'm going to head out now. You guys all good?"

Kye shifted closer to Tori, throwing an arm over her shoulders. "We're good. Thanks."

Oliver's gaze narrowed to where he was touching her. He could see the laughter in his friend's eyes. Could Kye tell Oliver was a second away from breaking his damn arm?

Luckily, Tori put down her sandwich and stood, walking toward him, saving Kye an injury.

Reaching up, she surprised Oliver by pecking him on the cheek. Christ, that small touch of her lips had him wanting more. Wanting to draw the woman into his arms and drag her upstairs.

"You really like him, huh?"

Tori's head swiveled around at Kye's words. "I do." Even though he was stubborn as a mule and damn good at pushing her away, he'd been sweet the last twenty-four hours.

His mood changes were kind of giving her whiplash, though.

She turned back to the sink and rinsed her plate. She was about to place it in the dishwasher when suddenly Kye was beside her, taking the dish from her fingers and doing it for her. "Not gonna lie. I'm a big fan of the single life, and I assumed Oliver would be in it with me for the long haul."

Tori's heart kicked. "Assumed? Past tense?"

"Yeah. Not sure that's the case anymore." He winked at her.

Warmth filtered through Tori. "Aren't you scared of what might happen if he trusts me and I'm not the person he thought I was?"

They had her memories but not her entire identity.

Kye was silent for a moment. "My gut tells me I can trust you. I'm rarely wrong."

Tori laughed, grabbing a glass from the counter and passing it to him. "Everyone's wrong sometimes."

"Guess I'm not everyone."

"None of you are," Tori mumbled. They weren't even close to being like everyone else.

Kye cracked a smile. "I never liked to fit the mold anyway."

"Does it bother you? What they did to you?"

"It bothers me that my brothers were put at risk. That they had drugs injected into their bodies, which could have gone a different way." He paused. "Those guys mean everything to me. If they'd died…" A menacing look crossed his face. The team joker temporarily missing.

She tilted her head to the side. "What about you? You could have died."

"I voluntarily became a Navy SEAL, knowing it was a dangerous job. Death doesn't scare me."

"But losing people you love does?"

"Yes."

His team was his family. And their lives meant more to him than his own. That was love right there.

Tori grabbed a towel and dried her hands. "Mind if I go upstairs and have a bath?" She was loving the deep tub in the bathroom connected to her room.

Kye headed into the living room, dropping onto the couch. "Go for it. If you hear the doorbell, it's the food I ordered from Joan's Diner."

"You just had a grilled cheese sandwich!"

He popped his feet onto the coffee table, looking totally relaxed in Oliver's home. "I didn't know the man was going to make me food. Was I hopeful? You bet. But I wasn't going to rely on it. And even if I did know, I probably still would have ordered more. This body doesn't fuel itself. It requires sustenance."

She smiled and headed toward the stairs. God, the man was a riot. "Okay."

"Want me to save you some fries?"

Tempting. But with the time she planned to soak in the tub, the fries would be dead cold. "No thanks."

Tori jogged upstairs and went to her bathroom, locking the door after her. What were the chances Oliver kept bath salts in his guest bathroom? Slim, but maybe...

Crouching down, she rummaged through the cupboard. When her hands slid over a small jar of salts, she almost thought her eyes were deceiving her. She shook her head. "Oliver, you surprise me."

Moving to the tub, Tori turned on the tap. It had only been running for seconds when the doorbell rang downstairs. She could just imagine Kye right now, the smile on his face as he collected his second lunch.

Chuckling to herself, she grabbed her phone from her pocket. Well, Oliver's phone, if she was being technical. She was about to place it on the side of the tub when a thump sounded from downstairs.

Tori froze. The thump had been loud enough for her to hear

up a set of stairs and over the running water. What the heck had it been?

Switching the tap off, she took a small step toward the door. "Kye?"

She didn't call his name loudly, knowing he would hear her anyway.

No response. No shouted words from downstairs that he was okay. Nothing.

Trepidation trickled down Tori's spine. The sound could be nothing...

But a couple more seconds passed and there was still no word from Kye.

Lifting the phone, she clicked on Oliver's number.

"Tori?"

She blew out a breath at his voice. "Hey, um, it might be nothing, but..."

Footsteps sounded on the stairs, causing her heart to jump into her throat. Heavy footsteps. They could be Kye's—but something told her they weren't.

"Tori, talk to me. What is it? Where's Cage?"

She took a calming breath. "I was about to have a bath when I heard a thump from downstairs. I said Kye's name, but he didn't answer. Someone's coming up now. I don't think it's him."

A loud curse echoed through the line. "Lock the bathroom door. I'm turning the car around."

A second later, the doorknob to the bathroom jiggled.

Tori jumped back, her gasp piercing the air. If the person was like Oliver, a locked door wouldn't stop them.

"Talk to me, baby. What's happening?"

She opened her mouth to respond, but the knob rattled a second time. She remained silent, waiting for the door to fly open. For Aiden or someone just as fierce to step in.

The knob went still. A beat of silence passed.

"They couldn't break the lock." She whispered the words, air whooshing out of her chest.

"Good. They're not altered. You should be safe until I get there."

Should be...nothing was certain though. Plenty of criminals could break bathroom locks.

"If they get in, be ready to fight."

Her muscles tensed, going into fight-or-flight mode. There was nowhere to run. She had no choice *but* to fight.

You've got this, Tori. "Okay."

There was a clinking noise from the other side of the door. It sounded like metal hitting metal. They were jimmying the lock. There was nothing she could do about it. Nothing but wait.

"They're going to get in." An odd calm settled over her as she whispered the words. Another curse sounded from Oliver. "I'm going to put you on speaker and set the phone on the counter."

The sound of an engine revving roared through the phone. "Dammit! Be careful, honey."

Tori did as she'd promised, then she bent and rummaged through the cupboard. She'd seen antiperspirant spray a second ago.

When it came into view, she grabbed it and removed the lid. Then she climbed onto the counter beside the door and waited. She'd have one shot. One chance to take him by surprise. If she failed, she would lose the upper hand.

More rattling. More clinking.

Then the door flew open. A man in a black sweatshirt with a hood over his head stepped into the small room.

Before he could take a second step, Tori sprayed the guy in the eyes.

He cried out, grabbing at his face.

She quickly shot a leg out, nailing the guy in the head. He fell sideways, slamming to the floor, a knife slipping from his fingers.

Jumping off the counter, Tori grabbed the knife before running out of the room and toward the stairs.

She'd made it to the top step when he pulled her backward before sending her to her stomach. The knife flew from her fingers, landing on the second stair, just out of reach.

Her arms were yanked roughly behind her back. When her injured wrist twisted hard, she cried out in pain.

Something was wrapped around her wrists. Something hard and plastic. She attempted to yank her wrists away but couldn't.

Though she wasn't about to stop fighting.

She tried pushing back against him, twisting around. It was impossible. The guy's weight pinned her to the floor, immovable.

He pulled tighter on what had to be a zip-tie. She whimpered as the plastic bit into her flesh. Cutting into her already injured wrist.

He breathed heavily into her ear. "Gotcha."

He pulled her to her feet. Still, she struggled. Kicking and writhing in his hold. He eased her down a step just as she threw her weight back.

The man stumbled, hitting the balustrade. Tori threw her head back, nailing him in the nose. The guy reeled back farther. Then she shot a foot backward, getting him between the legs.

It worked. He immediately released her. Unfortunately, in the process, he doubled over, shoving her down the stairs.

Tori had no hands to steady herself. No way to soften the fall. She tipped forward.

CHAPTER 19

*O*liver took a hard left onto his street, his hands clenched so tightly it was possible the wheel would crack beneath his fingers.

A man cried out over the line. There was the sound of body impacting body, followed by retreating footsteps.

"Dammit!" Oliver slammed his foot harder on the accelerator. Where the hell was Kye? How had this guy made it into the house and gained access to Tori?

If he hurt her...

Rage coiled through his body. The asshole would die.

While keeping the call on speaker, Oliver sent a message to his brothers. Marble Protection was close. If they were at work, they wouldn't take long.

Oliver slammed his foot on the brake outside his home. Jumping out of the car, he raced inside. The first thing he saw was Kye's still form beside the door. There was a heartbeat, and his chest was rising.

At the sound of movement on the stairs, he swung his gaze up to find Tori throwing her head back into a man's nose. When her leg flew backward, getting the guy between the legs, he bent over, pushing her forward, down the stairs.

Oliver reached her moments before her body hit the staircase, catching her in his arms.

"What the hell...?"

Oliver ignored the muttered words from the guy above. Racing down the stairs, he placed Tori gently on the floor. A growl tore through his chest when he saw the plastic cuff digging into her wrists. Cutting off the circulation.

He broke it with one tug.

At the sight of blood on her wrists, any speck of compassion for the attacker died. The asshole would pay. "You okay, honey?"

She swallowed, looking far from okay. Still, she nodded.

Eden ran through the door, his eyes alert, looking for the threat.

Oliver pressed a gentle kiss to Tori's forehead before turning to Eden. "Stay with her."

He didn't bother racing up the stairs. The guy wouldn't be getting away. He walked up slowly. Letting the anger boil in his gut and mirror on his face.

The guy was backing away. Through the hood, Oliver could only see his eyes. They looked scared.

He'd touched *his* woman. Hurt her. He would die for that.

The guy eyed the window.

Oliver shook his head. "Not gonna happen." Not a chance in hell.

"How the fuck did you move so quickly?"

He raised a brow, making it up the final step. "They didn't tell you? I'm barely human. I'm a predator. A killer. I could snap your neck in seconds. Or I could draw out the pain. Make you wish for death."

The asshole's heart pounded triple the rate it should. Good. He wanted the guy scared. Fear was a great motivator. The guy was tall and muscular, but he was human. No match for Oliver.

"You broke into my home. Touched my woman. Two mistakes that you'll pay for." Oliver took a step closer, reaching out faster than the guy could blink and yanking the hood off his head. "Who are you?"

He looked to be in his mid-thirties. His brown hair and eyes made him completely unremarkable.

He raised his hands. "I'm hired muscle, nothing else. Known for getting jobs done that others can't. I don't even know the name of the guy who hired me. But he offered me good money."

The man spoke the truth. It wouldn't save him though. "What was the job?"

Footsteps sounded behind him. He felt the presence of his brothers.

"To shoot the guy with the wrist tranq and take the girl. When a delivery guy arrived, I saw my opportunity. I wasn't told about *you*."

Of course not. Because then he wouldn't have taken the job.

Asher stepped to one side of Oliver. Luca to the other.

"What were you supposed to do with her?" Asher asked.

The guy swallowed, studying all three of them with trepidation. "Once I had her, I was to call the guy who hired me. He was going to tell me where to deliver her."

Smart. If the guy failed the mission, which he had, he had nothing but a number. Hylar had taken a risk employing an unaltered human. His lack of soldiers, and fear of losing any more, was evident. His weakness was bleeding out of him.

"Call him. Tell him it's done," Oliver said in a low, deadly tone.

A frown creased his brow. His eyes darted from Oliver to Asher to Luca. He didn't move.

"*Now.*" Luca's voice was harder. Louder.

"The guy will kill me!" Frustration mixed with fear on his face. He knew he was screwed either way.

Oliver almost smiled. "What do you think *we'll* do?"

When the guy continued to stand there, unmoving, Oliver

turned, grabbing the knife from the stairs before stepping into the guy's space, pushing the sharp tip to his stomach. The man was almost the same height as Oliver. Nowhere near as strong though.

"Remember what I said about wishing for death?" He spoke the words quietly enough that they wouldn't reach Tori's ears. "Hylar forgot to mention that you were stepping into the home of his enemy. A man who would do *anything* to track him down and end him."

Oliver trailed the knife up and paused at his collarbone, covered by a sweatshirt. He pressed it through the material, knowing he was breaking skin. "I'd say you have a more immediate threat than the man who hired you."

The guy instinctively reached for the knife.

With lightning reflexes, Oliver grabbed his wrist so tightly he felt the snapping of bones.

The guy cried out. "Fine! I'll do it."

Stepping back, Oliver watched as he reached into his pocket and pulled out a phone. He hit dial, then speaker. Speaker wasn't necessary, but the asshole didn't know that.

"Do you have her?"

The familiar voice of their former commander had Oliver fighting for calm. It was the voice of the man who had started the war and was continuing to keep it alive. If he was here, Oliver wouldn't hesitate to kill him with his bare hands.

"Yes. Where do you want me to deliver her?" To the guy's credit, the fear on his face didn't sound in his voice.

"I want to hear her."

There was a slight hesitation from the guy; Oliver was pretty sure that's what did it. "I knocked her out."

A moment of silence passed. "I don't believe you. Oliver, my boy, you there?" Oliver bit back a curse. "I know you are, so you can either talk or I can hang up."

Oliver's blood boiled. "Where the hell are you?"

"Ah. Nice to hear your voice. I think you'll find out soon enough, my son."

Oliver scoffed. "Son? You're the furthest thing from a father."

"Isn't a father, by definition, the man who created you?"

"Exactly why you're not a father to any of us, asshole," Luca said.

Hylar sighed. "I was hoping you boys would have come to your senses by now."

"Looks like you need a plan B," Asher said.

"Oh, I have one. And soon you'll find out all about it."

Oliver shook his head. "You've resorted to hiring thugs off the street. You're just wasting time. You'll never win."

When Hylar spoke again, there was a new edge to his voice. "I won't stop. *Ever*. That's what makes me so dangerous."

"And that's why you'll die," Luca added, not fearing the commander's words one bit.

There was a beat of silence. "But I won't. And what you fail to realize is that I don't need a whole army. Just a few capable men."

Well, a few capable men hadn't worked for him so far, had they? "What do you want with the girl?"

He actually chuckled. "All will be revealed in due course."

"Here's a tip, Hylar." Oliver spoke through gritted teeth, sick of the guy's riddles. "Whatever you want from us, whatever you think you're going to get, it's not gonna happen. Ever. Your death is inevitable."

"It's that backbone that I love so much. All you boys have it. When people urged me to destroy you, I couldn't. I need that on my side. And I'll get it."

Oliver blew out a frustrated breath at the man's stupidity.

"Do me a favor—get rid of the guy. He's a loose end I don't have time for."

~

SAGE TAPED the end of the bandage before sitting back. "It's waterproof, so showering won't be a problem."

That was a relief, since Tori could really use a shower right now. She wanted to wash away the feel of the guy's rough hands on her. Wash the entire attack away. Was that possible?

"My wrists are really taking a beating this week." Tori half-smiled, not receiving a return smile from Sage, Maya, *or* Quinn.

Sage nodded. "They are. Luckily, the cuts from the plastic cuffs are superficial so should heal quickly and without scarring. The sprain should heal within a week, too."

"Thank you. Not just for bandaging my wrist. Thank you to all three of you for coming over and taking my mind off the almost-kidnapping."

She shot a quick look at Oliver. He stood in the kitchen talking to Mason, Bodie, Kye, and Wyatt. They looked so serious and angry. Especially Oliver.

When his gaze clashed with hers, there was an intensity there she hadn't seen before. Tori sucked in a quick breath before looking away. "I'm glad Kye's okay."

Seeing him on the floor, so still, had not only made her scared for his life, but also feel beyond guilty. He'd gotten hurt because he'd been looking after her. Because he was there to protect her.

"He is," Sage said quietly.

Quinn leaned forward in her seat. "I think his pride's injured more than anything. He's been tranqed like that before."

Tori's eyes widened. "Really?"

Quinn nodded. "Mm-hmm. I felt so bad after it happened. It was by a woman I trusted, while he was watching me. She turned out to be Hylar's half-sister."

"Hylar's *half-sister?*"

Quinn nodded again. "Yep. And Hylar ending up ordering one of his guys to kill her."

What the hell? "He can't be that sadistic?"

"Unfortunately, he is."

Tori was almost too shocked. Who ordered a kill on their own flesh and blood? "The guy must be a psychopath."

"He doesn't have a heart," Sage said quietly.

Tori saw ghosts in the woman's eyes. "Have you met him?"

She nodded. "He took my brother, Jason. Had him held against his will for years. Even altered his DNA. Then Hylar kidnapped me, drugged Jason, and I almost died at his hands."

Tori's mouth dropped open. She didn't know what to say to any of this. "I'm so sorry." The words felt achingly inadequate.

Sage lifted a shoulder. "Jason's safe now."

"Good." Tori's eyes slid across to Maya, almost too scared to ask. "You haven't been touched by this, have you?"

The look that crossed Maya's face told Tori she had. Her heart sank.

"Hylar had a partner, Sinclair. After his men raided my work-place and killed my colleagues, he came after me. The guy injected me with something that could have killed me. I was lucky though. Instead of killing me, the drug fixed a defect in my heart. Doctors are now trialing the drug to see if they can use it to help more people."

Quinn blew out a long breath. "The one good thing to come out of the shit show."

Sage sighed. "What are we doing? We shouldn't be talking about this after what happened to you, Tori. We should be trying to take your mind off it all."

She shook her head. "I don't mind. Oliver doesn't tell me a lot." Because he hadn't trusted her. Did he trust her now? "It's gives me a better understanding of who I'm up against."

"I think it just takes Oliver time to open up to people," Maya said with understanding. "The guys feel a lot of pressure to protect each other. After how you met, he's probably just being overly cautious."

"Give him time," Quinn added. "The guy looks at you like you're the world."

He did?

At that moment, Oliver walked into the living room, the rest of the guys behind him. Everyone looked tired.

Sage stood, immediately going to Mason's side. Oliver took the spot she'd vacated on the couch. His body was visibly tense as he lifted her wrists and studied them.

"We'll get out of here," Bodie said, taking Maya's hand and leading her toward the door. "Call us if you need anything."

In less than a minute, the living room went from full of people to just Tori and Oliver. He still held her wrists, the frown on his face so deep it seemed the marks might be etched into his skin permanently.

"Does it hurt?"

She hated the uncertainty in his voice. "Sage gave me some wonderful pain relief. It took away the sting."

That didn't seem to ease his torment. "I'm sorry."

"Why are you sorry? You didn't zip-tie my wrists together and attempt to kidnap me."

A soft growl vibrated through his chest. "You should be safe in this house. Instead, someone got in, got past Kye, and hurt you. Almost took you to god knows where."

She placed her good hand on his cheek, tilting his head up to look at her. "You don't have anything to be sorry about. Nothing that happened today is your or Kye's fault. Kye didn't know the guy had some sort of tranquilizer strapped to him. And you saved me from falling down the stairs. From the guy taking me."

So much angst reflected back at her. "We're going to have to wear vests under our shirts or something from now on. Both times, Kye was shot in the chest. It shouldn't happen again."

That was smart. "What happened to the guy who broke in?"

"Don't worry about him. He's taken care of and won't bother you anymore."

She almost wanted to push for more information. But at the same time, she didn't. Not knowing was easier. And she trusted

Oliver. She grazed her fingers over the frown lines between his eyes. "I hate that you're so angry."

He dropped his head into his hands, scrubbing his face. "I'm sorry. Hearing Hylar's voice... You being hurt and almost taken. I want to kill every enemy we have, but I can't damn well find them!"

Her heart bled for the man. He was so tormented.

"What can we do to take your mind off it all?" *Her* mind immediately went to a place it shouldn't. Not just to sex. She wanted to hold him. Comfort him. Remind him that there was good in the world.

Oliver breathed out a heavy sigh. "Let's watch a movie."

She squashed her instant disappointment. "Sure. What should we watch?"

"You choose."

She knew he wasn't really into the idea. She doubted he would take in anything on the screen. But Tori would choose a movie. She would sit beside him and offer whatever comfort he'd accept.

Because Oliver had started to mean a lot to her. So much more than he should.

CHAPTER 20

*T*ori parked her car. The sight of Charlie running toward her usually caused a smile to stretch her lips. Today it didn't. Not after last night.

She'd had a mission. One job. And she'd failed. The failure wasn't an accident either. It was a judgment call.

There was no way she could have drugged Oliver. Not after spending the day with the man and getting to know him. He wasn't the bad guy they thought he was.

Tori lay her head back against the headrest for a moment. It brought up one giant question. How could Hylar, Samantha's boss, have gotten it so wrong?

Sighing, Tori opened her door. Her feet hadn't hit the ground outside when Charlie was already jumping on her legs. Crying out for a pat.

"Hey, boy. I missed you, too. Sorry I didn't come back last night." Instead, she'd spent it with a wonderful man. "I'm sure the sleepover with Sammy went well and she took good care of you."

Tori straightened before closing the car door. She shot a glance at her friend's car sitting in the driveway. Dread twisted her stomach.

She wasn't looking forward to having this conversation. She'd text her friend to let her know she hadn't gone through with the mission but *hadn't received a response. Now she was going to suggest to Samantha that her boss may have sent her after an innocent man.*

Stepping inside, she dropped the keys onto the entrance table while scanning the living room to the left. "Sammy, I need to talk to you." Tori headed down the hall to her bedroom. "I know you're probably mad at me. This is going to sound crazy, but Hylar's wrong. Oliver isn't—"

Tori halted at the sight of Samantha in her bedroom. Her friend was shoving clothes into Tori's backpack, looking frantic. Scared, even.

"What are you doing?"

Samantha didn't look up. "You have to get out of town."

Tori's feet remained glued to the floor. What the heck was going on? Was Samantha having some sort of episode? She had always been a bit eccentric, but this...

When Samantha tugged open the next drawer, throwing more clothes into the bag, Tori snapped out of her confusion and marched over to her friend. Grabbing Samantha's arms, she forced her to pause what she was doing.

"Stop. You're acting crazy. What's going on?"

Jesus, Samantha's limbs were shaking. There was a panicked, almost crazed look in her eyes.

"I got it wrong. I got it so wrong! And I'm so sorry I dragged you into this!"

What was she talking about? "Dragged me into what?"

Samantha scrubbed a hand over her face. "The people I'm working for..." Her breaths shortened.

"Sammy, you're working for the government on a secret project."

Silence. The silence stretched so long, Tori wondered if Samantha was ever going to reply.

"I thought I was. But I'm not."

A chill seeped into Tori's bones. She almost didn't want to ask the next question. But she had to know. "Then who are you working for?"

Samantha shook her head, tears gathering in her eyes. "It doesn't matter who they are. What matters is that they're not good."

She rummaged through her purse and pulled out a huge wad of cash. Holy crap, that had to be thousands of dollars.

Tori gasped as Samantha shoved the cash into her jacket pocket before zipping it up.

"This is all I could get my hands on. They're going to come for you, and they're going to come soon. You need to run. Don't access your accounts. Don't use your ID. Just disappear."

Had her friend completely lost her mind? "Samantha, you're scaring me. No one is coming after—"

"Tori, I found documents that I wasn't supposed to find. Information detailing everything." Her voice cracked on the last word. She swallowed. "You didn't do what they asked. Now you're a loose end— and they're going to kill you. I can't lose you. Please! You need to run!"

Fear churned in Tori's gut. "But Hylar—"

"Isn't who he said he is! And I should have seen it earlier."

Blood drained from Tori's face. Samantha was frantic. And dead serious. "If these people are so dangerous, then you need to run with me."

A tear spilled over Samantha's cheek. "I can't. What I've created for them...it's so dangerous. I need to fix this."

"No." There was absolutely no way Tori was leaving without Samantha. "You're just going to get yourself killed."

The idea had nausea rolling in Tori's gut.

With trembling fingers, Samantha yanked something else out of her pocket. "I took this a while ago. Just in case."

She shoved it into Tori's other pocket.

Christ, was that a gun? "Sam—"

"This is a tranquilizer, made especially for their kind. It won't kill one of them, but it will slow them down. Knock them out for a few minutes and give you time to run. When they wake, they'll be slow and weak."

When Tori said nothing, Samantha pulled her into a hug. "I love you like a sister. Stay safe."

Tori's eyes shot open.

Oliver's strong thigh cushioned her head, the sofa cushion beneath her legs.

The movie still played on the TV.

Samantha. She'd tried to save her. *Had* saved her. And Tori had let her friend drive away. Back to danger.

Guilt sat in her chest like a rock. Bearing down on her heart.

"Tori?"

For a moment, she didn't answer. She madly blinked the tears away, not wanting him to see her pain yet again. Slowly, she sat up.

Oliver studied her. "What is it?"

Tori swallowed the lump in her throat. "Samantha saved me. She gave me the tranq gun, the money, and told me to run."

And she had. Like a coward. Self-loathing clawed its way up her throat.

Oliver pushed a piece of hair behind her ear, his fingers grazing her cheek. Tori didn't feel deserving of the affectionate touch. "Did she say how she found out he wasn't who he said he was?"

"She said she found documents. She's really good with computers…" Her heart pounded.

"Did she tell you what she was working on?"

"No." Tori should have asked. There were so many things she should have done differently. "She said she couldn't run with me because she created something dangerous. She wanted to go back and fix it." When Oliver didn't respond, she shot him a quick look. He was still studying her. "I'm not lying."

His eyes softened. "I know."

"And whatever Samantha created, she didn't realize who she was creating it for. She probably died trying to right her wrong." Agony threatened to drown her. Tori had probably lost her best friend, just like she'd lost Charlie…and her mother.

"She could still be alive."

Oliver's soft words penetrated her haze of pain. So too did his soothing touch on the small of her back. His hand rubbing slow, firm circles.

"Maybe it wasn't the bullet to the skull that caused my amnesia. Maybe my mind was just trying to protect itself from losing everyone I love."

Was that possible? Every memory that returned to her seemed to be riddled with some sort of loss. She'd remember her love for someone, only to lose them all over again.

"I don't think so."

She glanced to the side, looking at the beautiful man beside her. "Why not?"

"Because you're tough. If loved ones were taken from you, you wouldn't be forgetting. You'd be searching for them. Keeping their memory close."

She shook her head, biting her bottom lip. "I shouldn't have let Samantha go."

He leaned forward, his face near enough for her to see the shards of emotion in his eyes. "Something tells me she wasn't going to let you stop her."

His lips were so close. "Kiss me. Make me forget for a moment."

If anything could ease her pain, it was a kiss from the perfect man beside her.

Oliver only hesitated for a second. Then his lips were on hers. Moving gently. Cherishing.

Awareness rushed from her lips to her core. Then need. Hot, all-consuming need for the man beside her.

Lifting her hands, Tori threaded her fingers through his hair, tugging his mouth closer. She didn't want slow and gently. She wanted fiery and passionate.

As if he heard her thoughts, Oliver gripped her waist. So firm and sure. His hold anchoring her to the spot.

The movie in the background drowned to nothingness as his

tongue slipped through her lips, tasting her. The fear and sadness from moments ago becoming distant memories.

The man's lips made her forget far more than any head injury could.

Rising up, Tori climbed onto his lap, a bolt of electricity shooting through her at the feel of his hardness pressing against her core.

Oliver tugged her shirt over her head. His lips only leaving hers for a second. Then they were back. Claiming her as his own.

His fingers grazed over her abdomen. She trembled under his touch. He slid his hands around to her back, quickly unclasping her bra.

Cool air brushed Tori's bare chest. When his hand captured one of her breasts, she whimpered. It was swallowed by his kiss.

God, this man made her feel too much. The bliss of his touch. The utter torture of needing everything all at once.

He caressed her breast. Stroked and massaged. Tori ground her hips against him. The need inside her rising like a wave in a storm.

Oliver tore his lips away from hers, brushing them across her cheek. Her neck. When he reached her breast, Tori's breath lodged in her throat. His tongue flicked across her hard nipple. Once, twice. Three times.

Tori writhed on his lap, gasping for air.

His mouth enclosed over the peak. Sucking the tight bud.

Her head lolled back, body on fire.

After endless minutes of torture, Oliver switched to the other breast. Licking and sucking, pushing her to the brink, then pulling her back.

She was so focused on the pleasure cascading from her breasts, she barely registered the hand unfastening her jeans, sliding inside, touching her core.

When his fingers glided between her folds, her body jolted. He grazed her clit in slow, seductive strokes.

She instinctively grabbed at his hair as a groan that she couldn't have held back if she wanted to, escaped her throat.

Yes. Yes to the man who surrounded her and the ecstasy he poured through her limbs.

He worked her, causing the ache inside to become almost painful. Then his finger entered her. She cried out at the welcome invasion. Latching onto his shoulders.

The combination of his mouth on her nipple and his finger inside her had Tori's entire body throbbing.

"Oliver..." she whimpered his name. Digging her nails into his flesh.

She tugged his head back to hers and kissed him fiercely, her hands sliding down his torso.

Tori undid his pants and reached into his jeans. She wrapped her fingers around him. Felt him thicken in her hold. She stroked him, enjoying the way his muscles tensed. The low growl from his throat.

Quickly, Oliver flipped them around so she lay flat on the couch. Within seconds, he had them both bare. Reaching for his wallet on the coffee table, he grabbed a condom and tore the foil packet open. Once it was on, he returned to her.

Her belly flopped at the incredible feel of his weight above her. At his hardness between her thighs. Tori widened her legs to give him more room.

He slowly pressed inside, pleasure blazing through her.

Once seated, Oliver stilled. They didn't move. They didn't speak. He looked at her like she was all that existed in his world. Like she belonged to him.

She did. Every little part of her belonged to Oliver.

His head lowered and he kissed her again. At the same time, his hips began rocking backward and forward.

Tori lifted her hips, meeting his thrusts. Deepening them. Small moans escaped her throat. Ripples of pleasure coursed through her core.

This man, this beautiful man above her, was intense and powerful and so damn important to her. He made her feel things she wouldn't have thought possible.

When his pace increased and his thrusts deepened, Tori arched her back. He took advantage, latching onto her throat with his mouth. Closing a hand around her breast.

He flicked his thumb over the peak.

Tori fell over the edge. She exploded, shattering into a million pieces, crying out his name.

Almost simultaneously, Oliver groaned. He thrust into her two more times before tensing. A guttural growl vibrating through his chest.

Tori was still throbbing around his length when their bodies went still, her heart hammering in her chest.

It was when his lips found hers again, to give her one final sweet kiss, that she realized she couldn't deny it. She loved this man. He had her heart—and there was no going back.

CHAPTER 21

*T*he ringing of his phone cut through Oliver's unconsciousness, snapping him from dead asleep to wide away.

Gently, so as to not wake Tori, Oliver slid his arm out from under her. Grabbing the phone from his bedside table, he left the room, noticing it was just after six in the morning.

He closed the bedroom door before speaking. "Jobs, what is it?"

"Grace Victoria Blake."

Oliver scrubbed a hand over his face. Maybe he wasn't as wide awake as he'd thought. Wyatt's words made no sense. "Who's that?"

"Tori."

That had his body stilling. His eyes shooting to the bedroom door. "You found her."

"Yep. After you mentioned Tori may be her middle name, I searched people with the middle name Tori, and variations of Tori, who lived in and around the area where she was found."

"You're sure it's her?" Oliver almost didn't want to believe it, in case they were wrong.

"Thirty years old, served two terms in the Army, mother died seven months ago from breast cancer and Grace inherited her house—which was located less than a mile from Gorman Falls, just outside the Colorado Bend State Park."

He ran a hand through his hair as he tread slowly down the stairs. "And Gorman Falls feeds into the Colorado River...where she was found." Oliver dropped onto the couch. "Can't believe you found her. Anything else pop up?"

"Nothing yet. And couldn't find anything on her friend Samantha."

Oliver nodded. He'd suspected as much. "Thanks, Jobs."

"You gonna tell her today?"

Definitely. It was her identity they'd just uncovered. She would want to know as soon as possible. "Yeah." He paused while he considered his next words. "And I've decided to stop fighting it."

"It?"

"My feelings for her. I'm done with trying to pretend they don't exist. I can't stay away from the woman. Even if I could, I wouldn't want to. Tori's mine. We fit together well." Too damn well.

"You trust her?"

"Yes." He was late to the party and should have trusted her earlier. But he was there now. "I can see and feel the goodness inside her."

"Took your time."

His friend wasn't wrong. He'd lost precious days that they could have spent together. They were days he'd need to make up to her.

"I know. But I got there in the end."

The subtle sound of the mattress dipping sounded from upstairs. Then light footsteps.

A few seconds later, Tori was downstairs. She was wearing his T-shirt, which drowned her.

One thought raced through his head.

Mine.

Lifting a hand toward her, he waited for her to come to him. When she moved closer, Oliver tugged her onto his lap and put his phone on speaker.

He pressed a kiss to her temple, enjoying the soft shiver that raced through her. "Jobs has some good news for you."

Her brows lifted. "I like good news."

Wyatt chuckled. "Well, then you'll love this. I found you."

"Found me?" A combination of confusion and hope crossed her face.

"Your name is Grace Victoria Blake, and you live near Gorman Falls in Texas."

Recognition lit Tori's expression. "Gorman Falls..." She rubbed her temple and her brows pulled together.

When she remained silent, Oliver tightened his hold on her waist. "What is it, honey?"

"I'm not sure...but I think that might be where I was shot. Near the top of the falls." She shook her head. "I just had this sudden memory of falling. The water flowing around me."

Oliver's jaw tensed. Those falls were over sixty feet high. "It's too high."

"The water at the base of the falls is pretty deep." Wyatt spoke through the line. "If she'd landed at the right angle, her body relaxed, she could've easily come out of the fall with no broken bones."

Tension coiled in Oliver's gut at the thought. It was Tori's soft touch on his shoulder that had his bunched muscles releasing.

"Adrien was only at partial capacity," Wyatt continued. "He may have assumed he either got the kill shot he needed or the drop into the water finished the job."

Just like that, Oliver's muscles bunched again. He was going to kill that asshole.

If what Wyatt suspected was true, then Adrien would have

reported back to Hylar that she was dead. When had they found out she wasn't? *How* had they found out?

Tori caressed Oliver's cheek. "What is it?"

"How did they know you didn't die? How did Hylar know to send a man *here*?"

Oliver already knew the answer to that, though. There was only one answer. Hylar had eyes on them. He had to. There were no cameras or listening devices in his house, the team did weekly sweeps. So was Hylar or one of his men close by? Watching from the shadows?

The idea had him holding Tori even tighter.

"We'll find out," Wyatt said with unrivaled certainty.

Tori nibbled her lip as she looked at the phone. "I want to go there."

"Where? Gorman Falls?"

"Yes. To my house," Tori answered.

He shook his head. "We can't guarantee it's safe—"

"There's no guarantee *anywhere* is safe. I'll be as safe as possible because *you'll* be with me. Please, Oliver! I need to see my home."

Christ, he hated the way her eyes pleaded with him.

Then she lowered her voice a fraction. "Also...Charlie would still be there. I need to bury him."

Goddammit. How the hell was he supposed to say no to that? "Okay. But I go in and check the place first. And if I say it's not safe, we leave. Period."

She sank into him, her arms going around his waist. A kiss pressed to his shoulder. God, the woman shattered him.

"I'll come," Wyatt said from across the line. "I'll give Kye a buzz and ask him to come too."

That was better. There was safety in numbers.

Oliver didn't think Hylar would be there waiting for her. But it was better to be safe than sorry.

He wasn't risking Tori. Not after accepting she was his.

~

FROM HIS PERIPHERAL VISION, Oliver caught Tori wringing her fingers together in her lap. They weren't even halfway to her house, and she looked nervous as hell.

Taking a hand off the wheel, he covered both her hands with his own. "Why are you nervous, honey?"

One hand slipped out from below his to cover his hand. "I'm nervous about finding Charlie. And about not remembering anything."

"Don't put so much pressure on yourself. Your mind will remember everything in due course."

She nodded but remained silent.

"Do you remember why you go by Tori rather than Grace?"

When he looked across, he caught her small frown. "I'm almost certain Samantha came up with the nickname. I can't quite remember why though."

"You can ask her when we find her." He squeezed the hand that remained below his. "Would you prefer me to call you Grace?"

She chuckled, some of the tension releasing from her shoulders. "No. I think that would be strange now. Tori feels right coming from you."

Good. He'd call her whatever she wanted, but Tori felt right to him too.

"I remember meeting you."

Oliver raised his brows, surprised. "Tell me about it."

"I was shocked by how good-looking you were. Shocked by how attracted I was to a felon." Oliver chuckled. "I remember noticing the crinkles beside your eyes when you laughed and thinking, 'What kind of bad guy has laugh lines?'" She dipped her head. "I even remember waiting for you to slip up. To drop the alluring smile. Say something that would expose your true nature."

Interesting. "But I never did?"

"You never did."

"What was the tipping point?" The point where she went from suspecting he might be good, to *knowing*.

"I could say it was a million small things. That would be the truth, because everything factored in. But there was something particular that stood out."

She paused. Oliver didn't say anything, knowing she'd speak when she was ready.

"At dinner, you asked about my mom. I was trying not to reveal any personal information, while also being careful not to lie."

Oliver frowned, remembering their conversation like it was yesterday. "You said your mom was a long way away. Unreachable."

"I did. And you reached across the table, touched my hand, similar to how you're touching it right now, and told me you were sorry. That a mother's love can't be replaced." Tori bit her bottom lip. "There was real emotion in your expression. Genuine empathy. I felt it on such a deep level."

After a quiet moment, she lifted a shoulder. "When I was putting the sedative into your wine, I couldn't shake your words. I remember the phone feeling heavy in my pocket. I was supposed to call Hylar once you were down. Let his men in to take you away."

His skin chilled at the thought of what might have happened. "But you didn't."

"But I didn't."

Oliver stopped at a red light. He turned his head and watched Tori, loving the way her face was so expressive.

When she turned her head to look at him, she smiled. "Why are you staring at me?"

Wasn't it obvious? "Just thinking about how beautiful you look."

A rosy-pink color entered her cheeks. Adorable.

"If I stared every time I was thinking about how good-looking you are, I wouldn't be taking my eyes off you."

Oh, that would be just fine with him. "I don't see a problem with that." In fact, he would probably prefer it. He didn't like her eyes on other guys, anyway.

Her smile grew. "Imagine how many doors I'd walk into. The milk I'd pour outside the cup."

Oliver shook his head. "Nope. I wouldn't let either of those things happen. I'd be your eyes, honey. And to make your life that much easier, I would carry you everywhere." Yeah, he was liking that idea.

Tori threw her head back and laughed, showcasing her long, delicate neck. "Okay. You can carry me everywhere and I'll stare at you all day. That won't be weird at all."

He scoffed. "I'd give up normalcy for you."

He'd give up a lot for the woman.

CHAPTER 22

*T*ori was bombarded with familiar scents the second she stepped through the door. Cinnamon, clove, nutmeg... maybe even a hint of vanilla.

Home. That's what it smelled like.

She stepped left into the living room, which opened to the kitchen. The space was small but homey.

So many memories hit her at once. Of her mother standing by the stove cooking dinner. Watering the potted plant by the window, which was now wilting. Even Charlie laying by the fire on cold winter nights.

This was where she'd grown up. And bit by bit, she was recapturing those memories.

Once the nostalgia settled, Tori took note of the state of the place. It was trashed. The coffee table was turned over, the beige couch slashed so severely it would be impossible to salvage. Even the cupboard doors in the kitchen had been pulled from their hinges.

An unexpected rage blasted through her veins.

A strong arm snaked around her waist as Oliver came to stand beside her. "You okay, honey?"

She should probably be sad that her belongings were destroyed. Belongings that had mostly been chosen and bought by her or her mother. She wasn't. She was *furious*. So damn furious that her skin tingled with the desire to hurt the person who did this.

"Why did they have to destroy everything?" Was shooting her into a river not enough?

Oliver pressed a kiss to the top of her head. "If your body had been found in the river, they probably wanted it to look like a murder-robbery."

Well, they would have achieved it. "I wish you guys had been here when they'd done this." If anyone could have stopped them, it was Oliver and his team.

"I dream about that shit," Kye muttered as he stepped into the room.

He and Wyatt had done a quick sweep of the house before she'd come inside. That's how she'd already known she wasn't going to like what she saw. Their faces had been tight with barely concealed anger.

She hadn't asked about Charlie yet. She'd been too scared of the answer.

"Was he..." God, she couldn't even say it. "Is Charlie in there?"

Her bedroom was behind where Kye currently stood, the door closed enough that she couldn't see inside. His features softened. "No."

No? So they moved Charlie's body?

She walked slowly to the bedroom, feeling Oliver's presence behind her. Sure enough, when she stepped inside, Charlie wasn't there.

For a moment, she didn't know what to think. She was relieved that his body hadn't been left to rot. But where was he? "Do you think he survived?" Her heart soared at the possibility.

"It's very possible. We can check with the park rangers and local shelters."

That was something. A small sliver of possibility that he was alive.

For the next half hour, the four of them searched her family home. She found photos—so many photos—of her mom, of Samantha, of Charlie lounging in the sun. Everything of true value to her was unharmed. And nothing else had been taken.

When every room had been thoroughly checked, she stepped back into the living room, feeling an odd combination of elated and defeated. She'd regained a ton of memories, mementoes... even her family home. But at the same time, had found, and remembered nothing to help the search for Hylar.

Tori hugged her waist. "I'm sorry I couldn't find anything helpful to you guys."

Oliver was in front of her in seconds. Wrapping his arms around her, pulling her against his chest. "There's nothing for you to be sorry about."

She smiled as he pressed a kiss to her forehead. He'd been doing that a lot today. Kissing her here and there. Light touches. She wasn't about to question it. She needed every one of them.

Then his gaze shot up to the ceiling, his jaw visibly tensing, before he quickly looked away.

Strange. He'd done that a few times in the last thirty minutes. Turning her head, she followed his gaze to the air-conditioning vent.

When she turned back to look at him, and he didn't volunteer any information, Tori had to ask. "What is it?"

He sighed. "There are cameras in your air vents, honey."

What?

Tori studied the spot where he'd just been looking. The vent was positioned in the center of the ceiling.

She moved underneath it. She couldn't see—

Her breath hitched in her throat. "No."

"Tori..."

Ignoring Oliver's warning, Tori grabbed the last remaining

unbroken chair and positioned it underneath. She shrugged off Oliver's hand, not sure if he was trying to stop or help her, but not wanting to take a chance on the former. Once she was stable, Tori studied the vent again.

She saw it. And her blood ran cold in her veins.

"I'm going to kill them." Her voice was low but deadly.

Oliver ignored her attempt to brush his hands away, instead taking hold of her waist and lowering her to the floor. When she attempted to pull away, he tightened his hold. "Tori—"

"I want to know if there's more."

She saw the tick in his jaw before he released her. She grabbed the chair but it was swiftly taken from her hands by Oliver. He followed her as she walked past Kye and Wyatt into the hallway. Shoving it under the air vent, she climbed up to study it.

Sure enough, there sat another camera, so small, and positioned so discreetly, it was almost invisible.

Without a word, Tori climbed down and systematically checked every vent in the house.

Cameras were everywhere.

She intentionally left the bathroom until last, not wanting to believe she'd find one there.

Climbing onto the edge of the tub, she studied the ceiling fan, ignoring Oliver's curse as he steadied her waist. When she spotted the camera she was looking for, Tori's mouth dropped open.

Even here? While she showered or lay naked in the tub?

This time, she didn't resist when Oliver lowered her to the floor. Her chest rose and fell in rapid succession. She felt both angry and violated. "They watched me in *here*? And in my bedroom..."

Nausea welled in her stomach.

Oliver tugged her back into the bedroom. His hand went to her chin, tilting it up, waiting for her gaze to meet his. That's when she saw it. The anger that mirrored her own. The outrage.

"I want to murder them for it. For touching your life at all. They would have done it because you were close to Samantha. To make sure she didn't say anything she shouldn't or question anything they didn't want her to question."

It made sense. It all did. It didn't make her feel any better.

For about the hundredth time that week, Tori wished she knew where her friend was. Whether she was safe. She leaned into Oliver, absorbing some of his strength. "Do you think we'll find Samantha?"

"We'll do everything we can."

That wasn't a yes. But it was the best he could do. She doubted he wanted to lie to her, but he couldn't say what she wanted to hear, either.

Her gaze went back to the ceiling. "Do you know how long it's been there?"

Samantha had been working for Hylar for years. She didn't want to think they'd been watching her that whole time.

Oliver stretched his arm up. The man was so tall, he easily reached the small camera, yanking it down.

The second the camera was released, liquid sprayed into Oliver's face.

His big body immediately dropping to the ground.

He'd barely hit the floor when the shattering of glass sounded from the living room.

A cry escaped Tori's lips as she dropped to her knees beside him. Oh god! His body was so still. Was he even breathing? "Oliver? Wake up! Please, wake up."

Nothing. Not a flicker of movement. He was out cold.

A war raged from the living room. The sound of fists colliding with skin, bodies being thrown to the floor. It was loud, echoing through to the bedroom, shaking the very walls.

Her desperate fingers clinging to his shirt, shaking his still body. "Oliver, you need to wake up! They've found us. Please!"

Her words were coated with panic. Not panic for herself. Panic for *him*. That he was vulnerable. Unable to defend himself.

"He can't hear you, love."

Tori jumped to her feet and spun around. Ice trickled into her veins. "Adrien."

She positioned herself in front of Oliver. To anyone watching, her attempt to shield him would look ridiculous. But an overwhelming need to protect the man she loved consumed her.

Adrien took a step forward. Tori's muscles tensed as another man showed up behind him.

"Anthony, you grab Oliver. I've got the girl."

No…

The two men moved forward at the same time. Tori kicked a leg out as Adrien went to grab her. He caught her foot easily. She quickly followed it up with a punch to the throat. He blocked that too, spinning her body around, holding her tightly against his front, an arm against her throat.

"Don't fight me, girl. I'm already angry about the tranq." His arm tightened, cutting off her air supply. "If it wasn't for Hylar, I'd be killing you right now."

Black dots began to obstruct her vision, her chest rebelling, screaming out for air. She was moments away from passing out when his arm suddenly dropped, causing Tori to fall to the floor.

Before she had a chance to recover, she was tossed over Adrien's shoulder. She could just make out Oliver beside her, hanging over Anthony's shoulder.

Adrien began to move. Tori kicked her legs out. Punched the man's back.

Nothing.

She lifted her head as he stepped into the living room. Violence and chaos. The room was flooded with it. Wyatt and Kye were fighting for their lives, outnumbered two to four.

Kye glanced up in time to see them stepping out the door. She heard his deep growl even after she was carried out of sight, into the late-afternoon sun.

When Adrien's feet hit the driveway, Tori's heart began to pound. If they got her and Oliver in the car, who knew where they'd end up—or if they'd ever be found.

She needed to make a last-ditch effort.

That's when she noticed the sheath on his hip—and what looked like a knife handle. The guy must have forgotten about it. Or assumed Tori was too scared to act.

Reaching down, she yanked the knife out of the sheath.

"What the—"

Tori plunged the sharp knife into the back of his thigh before quickly yanking it out. Adrien cried out, dropping her onto the driveway.

Air whooshed out of her lungs as she hit the ground hard. Ignoring the pain, Tori pushed to her feet. She'd only taken a step when fingers tangled in her hair.

Pain cascaded through her head as she was thrown several feet, the knife dropping from her fingers.

Her body collided with metal. A van. *Their* van.

She'd barely pushed to her elbows when she was yanked up by the arm. A fist immediately hit her in the face. Her head reeled back.

This time, she barely felt the pain. She barely felt anything. Her head felt light. Cloudy. Her legs wanting to give way but an unyielding hand continued to hold her up.

Adrien moved his face so close to hers, his breath brushed her skin. His features swam in front of her. "Next time you stab me, I stab back."

The edge of a knife pressed against her stomach, tickling her skin.

"Do you understand?"

Her eye felt heavy. She knew she was minutes away from

passing out. But when the knife pressed harder, just piercing her skin, she finally found her voice.

"Yes."

"Good." The knife vanished and she was carelessly thrown into the back of the van. Adrien climbed in after her, while Anthony got in the front.

When the van began to move, Adrien lifted a phone to his ear. "Disengage. We got them."

Oliver's body lay still beside her. She reached out her hand and touched his arm.

I'm sorry I couldn't save us.

She could only hope she'd get the chance to say those words out loud.

CHAPTER 23

*O*liver yanked on the metal chains at his wrists and feet. His arms were pulled behind his back, his ankles straddling a pole, the chain securing them on the other side, keeping him on his knees.

There was no give. Not even a little bit. The steel was seemingly unbreakable.

For the first time in what felt like hours, he stopped tugging. He breathed through the anger and frustration. The raw fear for Tori's safety. For the safety of his brothers.

Where were they? Had they gotten away? Were they hurt?

He needed some goddamn answers. No one was giving him anything. Not while chained to a pole in an empty fucking room.

Oliver cursed under his breath. His last memory before waking up in this room was of reaching up for the camera. What had happened between then and now? Whatever it was, it couldn't have been good. Not if this was where he'd ended up.

His muscles bunched at the idea that they'd gotten to Tori. That she was here, at Hylar's mercy.

He prayed that wasn't the case.

Jaw tensed, Oliver turned his head to look out the huge

window. It ran along an entire wall. He saw roads and the roofs of buildings. They were high up. He knew they weren't in Marble Falls but had no idea where they were.

The sun was only just rising, telling him it had been hours since he last saw Tori.

The room itself was white, almost sterile-looking. There was nothing else here but him and his chains.

What was worse, he could hear nothing. No heartbeats. No voices. Not even a damn footstep. He was either alone up here, or the walls were soundproof, even for him.

He was putting his money on the latter.

Oliver yanked on the chains again. The metal rattled just as the door to the room swung open.

Anger rolled off Oliver, his eyes narrowing at the sight of his greatest enemy. Hylar.

He came to a stop a few feet away. "Oliver, so nice to see you again."

Nice? It wasn't nice for Oliver. All he wanted to do was rip away from the chains and tear the guy apart. It was maddening.

Now that the door was ajar, Oliver could finally hear more than his own heartbeat. There were people out there. Not many. Maybe half a dozen.

Was she one of them? His brothers?

"Tell me she's far away from you assholes and my brothers are safe." Oliver snarled the words, his hatred for the man bleeding out of him.

Hylar didn't react to the tone or the words. "You haven't seen me in months, and even then, we hardly got a chance to talk. Don't you want to know how I've been? What I've been up to? There was a time when we were close."

Oliver didn't need reminding. "I don't have a fucking blind-fold on anymore."

And Hylar wasn't wearing a mask.

Hylar sighed. "That's disappointing. I've finally had to accept that you boys aren't coming back to me willingly. A bitter pill to swallow. And, to answer your question, your brothers are safe. For now."

At the intentional absence of any mention of Tori, Oliver's heart stuttered. "Where. Is. She?"

"These women have such holds over you boys." Hylar shook his head. "Doesn't that in itself show you what a weakness love is? This control that you let someone else have over you makes you vulnerable."

Oliver didn't need a lesson on weakness from this guy. His only weakness was that he hadn't seen the true Hylar from the start. Hadn't murdered him before Project Arma began. "Did you take her?"

Oliver was almost certain he knew. But he needed confirmation. His brain was struggling to accept this reality.

Hylar took slow steps over to the window, shoving his hands into his pockets. "She's here."

On the outside, Oliver didn't react. Internally, every part of him rebelled. Anger and fear hit him like a tidal wave.

She was here. At the hands of this animal…

"Adrien was supposed to kill her back at Gorman Falls. He thought he had," Hylar continued. "At first, I was angry at his oversight. Then it turned out to be a blessing in disguise."

Oliver was almost sure he wouldn't like the reason why. But he had to know. "What do you need her for?"

"Someone here cares about her. Someone who won't complete the job we need her to complete without some…incentive."

And Tori was that incentive.

Oliver's blood ran cold. What were they going to do? Threaten to hurt her if this person didn't comply? *Actually* hurt her?

Hylar turned back to Oliver. "I wouldn't worry about the girl, though. I'd be more worried about you."

More worried? Not a chance. "If that's the way you think my mind works, you never really knew me at all."

"Maybe that's true." His former commander walked toward him. "I chose you boys for your loyalty. I thought that loyalty would be unbreakable after what I gave you."

"Gave us?" Oliver sneered. "You injected us with drugs without our consent. You altered our DNA permanently. Planned for us to fight in your personal war regardless of our wishes."

Hylar looked confused. "I made you so much more than you ever would have been without me."

"You made us stronger and faster, but you didn't make us who we are."

The muscles bunched in Hylar's arms. The man wanted a thank you. No, he wanted Oliver to pick up a gun and fight the guy's enemies for him.

That wasn't going to happen. Ever.

"Luckily, I don't need your gratitude. I'll get your loyalty another way. It turns out, *any* mind can be manipulated with the right technology."

The guy made Oliver sick. "So, you've finally figured out a way to control us and I'm the first of my brothers to test the product."

Something akin to excitement crossed Hylar's face. "Yes." He took a step closer...so close, Oliver could almost touch him. What he wouldn't give to have a free hand right now. "This device is going to change everything. I'll finally be able to exact my revenge on the military for hanging my team out to dry. For leaving us in that godforsaken country for too damn long. To be tortured. Murdered."

"Yeah, Sinclair told us all about your capture in South Sudan. The thing is, you knew the risks when you became a SEAL."

Finally, some anger showed on the man's face. "You have no idea, *boy*. Imagine being captured. Watching your brothers die, one by one. Luca. Then Asher. Maybe they slice Eden's throat and force you to watch the life drip out of him. They all die. Bar you and Kye. No. They prolong *your* torture. It lasts months, bringing you to the brink of death without actually killing you." Hylar shook his head. "If you think you'd have one scrap of humanity left in you, one ounce of compassion for the people who sent you to that fate, you're wrong."

This was the real Hylar. The man he rarely let out. He almost looked psychotic. There were demons in his eyes. A deep-rooted anger that would likely never be extinguished.

The man's thirst for revenge was so much greater than anyone had realized. How the hell had Oliver and his team missed this side of him all those years?

Hylar blew out a long breath, seeming to recover from his rant. "That's why I've created an army unlike any the world has ever seen. A dozen men with the power of hundreds. Thousands." He paused. "Once I control you boys, don't have you trying to destroy me at every turn, I'll create more. My army will grow—and so will my power."

Oliver shook his head slowly. "But it won't. Because you won't ever achieve what you've set out to accomplish. We won't let you." Oliver leaned forward. "Ever."

Hylar's jaw clenched. Veins popped out in his neck. "If you weren't the useful soldier you are, you'd be ten feet underground right now. All of you."

Oliver lifted a shoulder. "Maybe that's *your* weakness. You created something you could never destroy. Instead, allowing it to slowly destroy *you*."

Even tied to a pole, with no idea where he was, Oliver still believed that they would destroy Hylar and his work. Good would prevail and their former commander would die. The guy would never get his revenge.

"The second I created you, you became property," Hylar sneered. "You breathe because I allow you to breathe. You live and love because I've given you that freedom. The moment you chose to hunt me instead of joining me, I started planning. That planning is finished." Hylar turned his attention toward the door. "Bring her in."

The bravado left Oliver in a second, replaced with cold dread at the possibility of seeing Tori. How would she look? How badly was she hurt?

But when Carter entered the room, he didn't have Tori. He dragged another woman behind him. A woman with blond curls escaping a hairband. Her dirty clothes looked like she'd been wearing them for weeks.

When she raised her head, anger ripped through Oliver's chest. Her face was covered in black-and-blue bruising. Dried blood spattered her skin.

She'd limped behind Carter as he dragged her. Her breaths were shallow and strained, indicating she likely had a cracked rib.

If Oliver hadn't been sure before, he was now. These men were the absolute scum of the Earth. "What the hell is wrong with you?"

Carter chuckled. "I knew he'd have a fit at the sight of her."

Oliver struggled against the chain, hearing the first small protest of the pole. Fucking animals. The lot of them.

"This is Samantha," Hylar said, not paying any attention to Carter's amusement or Oliver's rebellion.

Oliver's eyes went back to the woman. Samantha. Tori's friend. Her best friend.

If the woman was important to Tori, she was important to *him*. That made his muscles tense further.

She studied Oliver. "Who is he?" Even though she looked beaten and defeated, her voice was firm and strong.

Hylar didn't look at her as he spoke. "He's the man you're going to build the microchip for."

Her eyes narrowed to slits. "You know I'm not going to do that."

"Oh, but you will." Hylar walked over to the woman. Wariness misted her eyes, but to her credit, that was the only sign of her fear. She didn't pull back and her expression didn't change. "I know you wouldn't care if we hurt him. A stranger. And you've proven you don't care what we do to *you*." Oliver's hands clenched at that statement. "But fortunately, I have someone you *do* care about."

Oliver's stomach cramped. He thought he might be sick at what he suspected was coming next.

He hoped he was wrong. God, he'd lay down his life to be wrong. But he knew he wasn't.

Hylar turned to Oliver. "This is why love is a weakness. It makes you agree to do things you would never otherwise do." There was a small pause. "Adrien."

Adrien stepped into the room, a body hanging over his shoulder. She wore just a bra and underwear. And she was completely limp.

Tori.

Adrien dropped her onto the floor like a sack of potatoes.

Oliver's world narrowed to pinpoint accuracy. He couldn't hide the pain from his face if he tried. She was pale. Her heart rate slow. Her left eye black and almost swollen shut.

"You fucking assholes!" Oliver went wild. Pulling and wrenching at the chains. He used every ounce of strength he had and still didn't get anywhere. "What the hell did you do to her?"

"We knocked her out." Adrien lifted a shoulder. "Then she woke up, so we knocked her out again. I hear head injuries aren't good after suffering from amnesia."

Oliver was going to kill him. Tear him apart bit by bit.

"So, we know what Oliver thinks," Hylar said dryly. "What about you, Samantha?"

Oliver watched Tori for another moment, the ache in his body only increasing. When he finally turned his gaze to Samantha, it was to see the fear she'd been trying to mask moments before now showing.

No. Not just fear.

Downright terror.

Carter shoved her. She fell forward but caught herself before hitting ground. "Hylar asked you a question, bitch."

"How do I feel?" Her bottom lip trembled before she took a breath and straightened. "Scared. Because I know you're going to make me watch my best friend be tortured—since I'm not going to do what you're asking."

CHAPTER 24

$\mathcal{P}$ounding jackhammered through Tori's head. She scrunched her eyes shut tighter as she curled her body into a ball to protect herself from the cold.

Groaning, she hugged her waist. It took her foggy brain a moment to realize she was touching bare skin. Was she naked?

At the sound of rattling chains, Tori's eyes slowly slid open.

People stood around her, but she couldn't quite work out who. They were a blur of shapes. She blinked a few times, trying to focus on her surroundings. To connect the shapes to people.

Finally, her eyes landed on someone familiar. Oliver. He was chained to a pole. His shirt torn and dried blood dotting his body.

A bolt of panic shot through her.

When her eyes lifted to his face, she noticed it was contorted with rage. A wild rage so much worse than anything she'd ever seen before.

Bits and pieces of her last memory began to filter back. Oliver pulling the camera from the ceiling. Adrien taking her. Taking Oliver.

Her breath caught as she swept her gaze across the room. When she saw Hylar, she suddenly remembered the last time she was in his presence. Recalled the man handing her Oliver's file. Explaining her assignment.

The memory hit her full force.

She'd been so damn trusting.

Swallowing, she looked toward Adrien. He wore the same menacing expression on his face as every other time she'd seen him.

She glanced over at the two people on the side of the room. A tall man she remembered seeing on Wyatt's computer stood there, but she barely paid him any attention. Not when she saw who stood beside him.

"Samantha," Tori whispered her friend's name, a strange mix of relief and terror inside her. Relief that her friend was alive. Terror at who currently held her, the state she was in.

Oh god, what have they done to you, Sammy?

Tori pushed into a sitting position, unable to look away from her friend.

Tears misted Samantha's eyes. "I'm sorry."

Sorry? *Tori* was the one who'd let her friend return to these psychopaths.

"Sammy?"

Before Samantha could respond, Hylar shouted, "Daniel."

A second later, a tall man stepped into the room. Another man from the images on Wyatt's computer. He held some sort of belt in his hands.

"Don't even think about putting that on her." Oliver spat the words at the man, his muscles bunching as he rebelled against his restraints.

"Unfortunately, Samantha hasn't left us much choice," Hylar said. "She destroyed all the chips she'd already made, as well as the memory drive where the information was stored. Thus far, she's refused to rebuild any of it for us. This might change her mind."

Despite the fear and desolation of the moment, Tori couldn't help but be proud of her best friend. Her courage and strength were admirable.

Now Tori had to be equally strong. Because Hylar couldn't get his hands on whatever Samantha had created.

Hylar's gaze remained on Samantha for another beat, waiting for her to give in. When she continued to remain silent, looking unbelievably pale, Hylar sighed before nodding to Daniel.

The man walked toward Tori slowly. Every part of her wanted to pull back. To run away. But there was nowhere to go. Nowhere to hide.

Growls and curses tore from Oliver as he continued to struggle. They seemed to get louder with every step Daniel took.

He kneeled in front of her, strapping the belt around her stomach tightly, just below the rib cage. Tori didn't fight him. It wasn't a fight she'd win.

Once the belt was in place, Daniel headed back across the room, passing what looked to be a remote to Hylar on his way.

Samantha whimpered from across the room. The pained sound made Tori's heart hurt.

Hylar fixed his gaze on her once again. Samantha's gaze remained on Tori. "That high-voltage shock that went straight to your kidneys...that excruciating pain that you still have nightmares about...that's what your friend is about to go through." He paused. "You can stop this."

Tori's breaths shortened, fear she couldn't ignore crawling up her throat. She twisted her neck, noticing the two metal prongs on the belt, positioned on her left side below her kidneys.

Swallowing, Tori looked back to her friend to see a tear sliding down her cheek. There was so much sorrow in her eyes. "Tori." Samantha didn't even sound like herself. "If I do what they ask, it's not just us who will be in danger. It's the entire country… the world. *No one* will be safe."

Tori swallowed, fear now a living, breathing organism inside her, but she couldn't let her friend see. She couldn't allow Samantha to give this psychopath more power.

She whispered the words she knew she had to say. "Don't do it, Samantha. Stand your ground. I'll be okay."

Without warning, a pain like nothing she'd never felt surged through her body. It almost felt like she was on fire. Utter agony pierced through her.

Tori tried to scream but all she managed was opening her mouth. The burning stole her ability to make sound. To breathe. Her body seized and convulsed. Her bones feeling like they were breaking.

Just when she thought it would never end, when she thought it might actually kill her, it stopped.

Tori dropped flat to the floor. Exhaustion weighing her body down, making it impossible to lift a single limb. Her heart pounded fast and painfully in her chest.

In the background, Tori heard Samantha's sobs. Oliver's growls and yells. The chains rattling loudly.

She didn't have the energy to tell them she was okay. The truth was, she wasn't. The pain had been out of this word. And the knowledge that there was more coming…it almost made her wish for death.

ANGER, red and hot, raged through Oliver's body as Hylar pressed that goddamn button for the third fucking time. Tori convulsed on the floor, her face frozen in anguish.

All the while, he was chained to a fucking pole.

Each shock lasted eight seconds. Each of those seconds felt like a lifetime.

The aftereffects lasted longer than the shock itself. Minutes on end. The incapacitation, the shaking...

He needed to end this now.

Tori's shaking form had his entire body rebelling.

The asshole would do it again, too. Hylar didn't care about her life. He only cared about getting what he wanted.

Oliver turned to Tori's friend. She was the only one who could stop this. "Tell them you'll do it, Samantha! Whatever it is they want you to make, make it. We'll fix it later."

Her face was red from crying. Tears still streamed like a river down her cheeks. She almost looked like she was ready to give in. She opened and closed her mouth. Yet those words he needed to hear, the words *Hylar* needed to hear, never sounded.

"Samantha—"

"Don't do it." Tori's weak voice cut through Oliver's. Her words almost unintelligible. "Don't, Samantha."

No!

Oliver almost yelled his next words, wanting to drown out anything else Tori might say. "If they keep doing this, her heart will give out! She could die right here in front of us. Do you want to watch your friend die? Do you want that on your conscience?"

The torment that flashed through Samantha's eyes was exactly what Oliver needed. He needed her to feel the heartache of losing Tori. The guilt. It was the only way.

"Don't be the reason your best friend is murdered."

He was being an asshole. But he had to be. Oliver couldn't let this continue for another second.

"Sammy." At the sound of Tori's whisper, Samantha turned back to her. "Don't."

A look passed between the women. Words were spoken without being voiced. A silent agreement that Hylar wouldn't be getting what he wanted.

Fuck! Oliver wanted to punch something. He wanted to tear down the entire damn building.

Oliver switched his attention to Hylar, hating the way the guy's thumb hovered over the button. "She's not going to agree, Hylar. You need a new plan. Electrocute me instead."

The asshole almost seemed amused by the suggestion. "Why would I do that?"

"Because Samantha will only listen to Tori—and Tori loves me." She hadn't said it. But he loved *her*, and he was pretty damn sure she felt the same. "Zap me until I'm on the brink of death if you want. Tori will convince Samantha to build your microchips."

There was a small whimper from Tori. The softest cry. "No…"

Hylar was silent.

Good. The man was thinking about Oliver's words. Considering them. Oliver needed him to say yes. Needed to take away Tori's pain and redirect it to himself.

Oliver straightened his spine. "You want to control me? This is your chance. Hurting me hurts *her*, way more than torturing her ever will. Electrocute me, waterboard me, fucking stab me in the gut—the worse, the better."

He could hear Tori's ragged breaths. Her accelerated heartbeat wild in her chest. He didn't look at her. He couldn't handle the pain that was no doubt on her face.

Finally, Hylar turned to Daniel and nodded.

Air whooshed out of Oliver's chest. The relief was so intense if he hadn't already been on his knees, his legs would have given out.

Daniel kneeled in front of Tori and removed the belt. Her hand lifted slightly, only to fall straight back to the ground, like she wanted to stop him but was too weak.

It'll be okay, baby. I've got you.

Oliver wasn't scared of pain. He'd felt enough of it in his life.

Usually, he would internalize his pain. During his time as a SEAL, he'd learned to switch off that part of his brain when he needed to.

He had no intention of doing that right now.

No. He would be showing every single emotion. He needed Tori to be worried. To convince her friend to stop this. Scream at her.

Because if this didn't work, if Tori didn't convince Samantha to do as they asked, Hylar would turn his attention back to her eventually. And the next form of torture would be worse than this one.

Daniel strapped the belt below Oliver's ribs.

Carter laughed. "This just keeps getting better. No need to wait in between shocks, Commander."

Hylar sighed. "Remember, son. You asked for this."

Then his finger pressed down on the button.

An intense shock ran through Oliver's body. It felt like his organs were being squeezed in his chest.

Tori's cries echoed through the room. She sounded just as pained, if not more so, than she had minutes ago.

Oliver gritted his teeth and allowed the cry that was on his lips to unleash. He kept his head up, needing her to see what was happening.

Endless minutes ticked by. Every one of them riddled with red hot pain.

When the shock eventually stopped, Oliver's head fell forward. His limbs continued to shake.

"Maybe we'll dampen his body." Hylar's voice just penetrated Oliver's pain fuzzed mind. "Test whether his organs can withstand the combination of water and electrocution."

Shit. That could kill him.

Tori sobbed. "No…please, god, no! He won't survive."

Oliver hated hearing her panic. Other than sheer exhaustion, sorrow for Tori was all he felt.

The asshole chuckled. "Maybe. It would kill any *normal* man. We'll try this another time first, shall we?"

Tori screamed when the electricity returned to his body.

Oliver arched, throwing his head back. The pain was out of this world. Breaths were no longer making it into his chest.

"Please stop! You didn't even give him a minute of rest! You're going to kill him!"

"Tell Samantha to do it."

Oliver could barely make out the conversation around him. The haze of torture continued. He began to wonder if two shots in such close succession *would* in fact kill him...

"Samantha, do it! Please! I can't watch him die. Oh god, please!"

Finally, the electrical blast ended. But the pain remained. The involuntary spasms now so intense, the metal chains rattled against the pole.

"Let's get some water in here."

Footsteps and Tori's hysterical cries sounded.

Before the water arrived, Hylar hit the button again. Oliver didn't have time to tense before the electricity returned. He actually felt like his body was beginning to shut down. The pain wasn't registering quite so much. An odd fog had begun to seep into his mind.

The eight seconds felt like time stood still, then dragged out bit by bit.

He was vaguely aware of the agony almost bleeding from Tori. She was begging her friend.

This was what Oliver had wanted...yet his world of hurt was too intense to appreciate it.

When the electrical wave finally ended, Oliver's head fell forward once again. He was bent at an odd angle, unable to hold any of his weight.

"Samantha...please," Tori sobbed. "I can't lose him. Trust him to fix this later. Trust his *team* to save us. They will. I promise! Please."

There was a small pause. Someone entered the room, the sound of water sloshing in a bucket.

Tori whimpered. "Please, Sammy."

Then, in a low, almost regretful voice, Samantha said the words everyone was waiting to hear. "I'll do it."

CHAPTER 25

*T*ori fell to the floor as Carter shoved her into the cage. She barely spared a thought to the pain of her hip colliding with concrete, instead moving straight across to Oliver's still form. He was on his side but didn't move a muscle.

Christ, why hadn't he woken?

Dropping to sit beside him, placing her shaking fingers at his neck, Tori checked his pulse. Steady. A lot steadier than her pounding heart.

Some of the tension released from her muscles.

With her left hand, she grazed the side of his face. Seeing him like this had razor blades slashing at her insides.

She lowered her temple to touch his. "I'm sorry."

So damn sorry that he'd redirected the pain from her to himself.

A shiver racked her body. She still only wore her underwear and a bra. The room was far from warm. And exhaustion weighed on her. Exhaustion from the torture she'd been subjected to. The fear. The panic.

Angry red welts burned on her left side. Anytime something grazed against them, her body flinched. But she didn't care about any of that. All her concern was for the man on the floor. And Samantha. Where was she?

Tori lifted her head to study the bars that made up the cage. Standing tables and a laptop sat on the other side. From the window, she could see they were still somewhere high up.

At some point, Carter left the room, leaving just her and Oliver.

Pushing down the anxiety trying to etch its way up her throat, Tori was about to curl herself into Oliver's large body when the sound of a door opening pulled her attention. Looking up, she saw Samantha enter the room, trailing behind Daniel.

He tugged her by the arm, his fingers clearly digging into her flesh. The man only stopped when they arrived at the standing desk with the computer.

"You have no Wi-Fi," the guy growled as he released her arm. "You do as Hylar asked. I'll be standing over there watching. Got it?"

Tori saw the tensing of Samantha's jaw moments before she nodded.

Her fingers moved across the computer keys. Tori began to wonder if her friend was ever going to look at her. When another few beats of silence passed, she couldn't wait any longer.

"Samantha..."

Tori saw her pause. A tense frown marring her brow before she turned to look at her.

Her friend looked tormented. Like she was drowning in her own guilt.

What Tori wouldn't give to be able to touch her. Wrap her arms around her friend and pull her close. She shook her head. "Don't. Don't blame yourself. You were deceived. You never would have involved me if you knew the truth."

Tears gathered in Samantha's eyes. It hurt Tori's heart. "I should have seen the truth. I hate myself for dragging you into this." She sucked in a ragged breath as she turned back to the screen. "For what I've created."

Tori attempted to stand, but exhaustion weighed heavy, her legs giving way. Her body ached and rest called to her. But this was the first time she'd talked to her friend in over a month. "We're going to fix this."

Samantha's fingers began moving over the keys again. She took a moment before answering. "The cage you're in is electrified. Oliver won't be able to get out and help either of us. Daniel is behind me, watching everything I do. Pete and Anthony are downstairs, watching the exits. Hylar, Carter, Adrien, and Kip are nearby." Finally, she looked up again. "It would be hard for us to prevail."

Hard. But not impossible.

Had her friend said that intentionally? She'd always been optimistic. So much more optimistic than Tori.

But the woman standing across the room looked different from the one Tori was used to. There were ghosts in her eyes. A deep-seated pain that hadn't been there before.

"Are you okay?" Tori asked quietly, almost not wanting to know, but at the same time, *needing* to know everything.

Another shiver shook her body. She wrapped her arms around her waist, trying to ward off the cold and exhaustion. She gave herself a little shake, needing to stay awake. Talk to Samantha. Wait for Oliver to wake.

"You should sleep," Samantha said quietly, continuing to work.

"You didn't answer my question."

A minute passed of Samantha working. A minute of no words.

"He's cute," she finally said, nodding her head toward Oliver. "He really cares about you, too. I like that."

Samantha wasn't going to answer. She knew why. Her friend *wasn't* okay. Not even close. What had they done to her?

A crippling guilt hit Tori hard. Why had she let her friend go back all those weeks ago? Why hadn't she forced the woman to run with her?

Swallowing the regret, Tori looked down at Oliver. "I love him. I need him to be okay."

"Hylar won't let him die. Not with what I'm making for him."

Tori looked up, knowing that whatever it was, it had the potential to change everything. "What are you making?"

Samantha's fingers continued to fly over the keyboard. If she stopped, Tori had no doubt Daniel would be on her, forcing her to continue. "It's a human microchip. I designed it to be inserted into the shoulder blade. Signals are sent to the brain. Then, certain people can control the host. Take away their free will."

A loyal soldier. Just what Oliver's former commander wanted.

The idea was terrifying.

"They'll stop this, Sammy. I promise."

"They" being Oliver's team.

She wasn't sure if that was a promise she should be making. But there was so much desolation in the room. She had to believe that saviors were coming.

Samantha's fingers paused. When she looked at Tori, there was a flash of her old friend. "I've missed you."

For the first time since arriving in this hell, a small smile tugged at Tori's lips. "You have no idea."

Tori's eyes began to shutter again. The welts on her skin throbbed and her skin was icy.

Samantha, always so observant, noticed her expression softening. "Sleep, Tori. Snuggle into that beautiful man of yours. Borrow his warmth. And try not to worry."

Not worrying would be impossible. Still, Tori's body seemed to have a mind of its own as she dropped to the floor. She shuffled her back against his stomach, tugging his arm over her side.

Her eyes fluttered shut, too heavy to remain open. His warmth immediately heated her. And if she tried really hard, she could almost convince herself they weren't here, in the depths of danger, completely vulnerable.

THE SOUND of movement had Oliver's eyes snapping open. His muscles immediately tensed at the sight of Tori curled into a ball in front of him. Her body was completely still, apart from the soft rising and falling of her chest with each breath.

He touched her skin. Damn, freezing.

Tugging his shirt over his head, Oliver lay it over her chilled body. It was torn, but better than nothing. He wished like hell he had a hoodie. Something warmer he could give her. He took a moment to listen to her heartbeat. Normal. So too were her breaths.

But she was so still...

"She's sleeping."

Oliver's head shot up at the female voice from across the room. Before his gaze reached her, he noticed the cell-like bars surrounding him. They ran from floor to ceiling.

Hylar had put them in a damn cage.

When he looked beyond the bars, it was to see Samantha working at a standing desk. She had a light pointed at the table in front of her and an open laptop.

Creating the weapon Hylar had requested. Because that's what it was. A weapon. Against Oliver. His team. Against the whole damn world.

Oliver swept his gaze behind Samantha, seeing Daniel standing by the door. He watched the woman, a scowl on his face and a gun strapped to the holster on his waist.

This space was bigger than the other one. Various doors led off of the room, indicating it may be a foyer. They were still high up though, no doubt on the same floor.

Samantha spoke without looking up. "Tori was exhausted."

He looked back to Tori, sweeping some hair out of her face. God, he hated that she was here. Hated that they'd hurt her.

His body yet again tensing at the memory of what they'd done.

I'll make it up to you, baby.

Pressing a kiss to her head, Oliver stood. "How long was I out?"

"It's about five in the afternoon, so a long while. Maybe ten hours."

Damn. They'd really wiped him out.

Not that he felt any pain now. His body healed quickly. There wasn't even a mark on his skin where the electricity had hit him. He hadn't missed the welts on Tori's side, though.

He walked over to the bars and studied them. Lifting a hand, he was about to touch the metal when Samantha's words stopped him.

"I wouldn't do that if I were you. Unless you want high-voltage electricity coursing through you again."

His hand dropped to his side. Of course, Hylar had wired the cage. Oliver should know better.

He shot a look across to the window. "Where are we?"

Daniel smirked. "Doesn't matter. Those asshole brothers of yours won't find you."

Samantha's lips thinned. "Killeen. They used to pick me up from my house and drive me here. The windows were tinted. For two years, I had no idea where this building was." There was a slight pause. A shot of pain crossed her features before she quickly cleared it. "I thought I was working on a secret military project. So I didn't ask any questions."

He could hear the remorse in her voice. The woman felt guilty. Maybe even a bit silly. For not asking more questions, for not realizing the truth sooner. For creating something for people she shouldn't have.

He watched her fingers fly across the keyboard. "I'm surprised they trust you with a computer."

"It's just to get the program I tried to destroy back up and running. There's no Wi-Fi connection." For the first time, she shifted her gaze away from what she was doing and looked him straight in the eye. "I couldn't do anything to help you, even if I wanted to."

Without moving her head, her eyes darted to the side before returning to Oliver. They lingered on him for another beat before lowering.

Outwardly, Oliver didn't react. Internally, his mind was working. She'd just told him something important without actually telling him.

There *was* something she could do. But only if Daniel wasn't watching the computer screen. What, exactly, Oliver wasn't sure. Tori had mentioned how smart her friend was. Maybe she'd found a way around whatever firewalls they'd put in place.

"I'm creating this for them to use on you," Samantha said, fiddling with a tiny device on the desk. "Once this is done, and they can find someone to replicate my work, they won't need me anymore."

Which could be soon. At that point, they wouldn't need Tori either.

At the change in breathing behind him, Oliver went to Tori and kneeled in front of her. She snuggled under the shirt, curling herself into a ball.

Oliver touched her cheek. "How long has she been out?"

"Almost as long as you," Samantha answered. "She was really wiped out, so I wouldn't be surprised if she slept for a while longer."

Oliver was about to scoop Tori into his arms, give her some much-needed heat, when he heard the sound of the door opening. By the cadence of the footsteps, Oliver already knew who it was.

Clenching his jaw, he stood and turned. Hylar had entered, Carter trailing behind him.

Hylar stopped behind Samantha, studying the screen. Oliver didn't miss the small shudder that rocked her body. "How much longer?"

Even his voice had Oliver wanting to murder the guy. If there weren't bars separating them...

Samantha kept her gaze down. "Maybe another hour?"

"Fine. An hour. No longer." Hylar placed his hand on Samantha's shoulder. There was the slightest wince from her.

A hot, angry breath escaped Oliver. "Hey, asshole. Wanna tell me what you and your circus crew plan to do to me?"

Hylar's hand dropped, gaze shifting to Oliver. "Samantha here has created a human microchip. The first of its kind. When inserted correctly, and orders are given by the right person, this chip takes away a person's free will."

Oliver didn't need to be told who that "right person" was. "You think I'm going to fight for you?"

One side of Hylar's mouth lifted. "I know you will." He moved closer to the bars. "You'll finally become the loyal soldier I always hoped you'd be. If I tell you to kill the woman behind you, you won't bat an eye. You'll walk right up to her and snap her neck."

It was an effort not to react to his words. To not flinch at the image he created. "If you think it's possible for me to harm a single hair on her head, you have no idea who I am."

He chuckled. "But I do. You're a man with immense potential. I gave you more power than most men could ever dream of possessing. Unfortunately, you have a weak mind. Something I realized too late. You let emotions and relationships and the idea of love dictate what you do."

"Should I be more like you? Willing to kill family?"

"Yes. It's called dedication to a cause. Nothing will stop me from achieving my goal. From building my army and getting my revenge."

Oliver ground his teeth. The man wasn't just an asshole. He was a sociopath.

Hylar indicated behind him with his head. "Look at Samantha. It goes against everything in her to build what she's creating. And yet, there she is, making the device she doesn't want to make. Recapturing information she tried to destroy. Why? Because she loves her friend, and her friend loves you. If that isn't the greatest example of pathetic, I don't know what is."

Oliver looked over Hylar's shoulder. "How does it feel, Daniel? To know that you're merely a tool in another man's war? A way for him to exact revenge on his enemies."

Daniel's expression didn't change. "Hylar's given me everything. Strength. Speed. Purpose."

Oliver laughed, even though there was nothing remotely funny about any of this. "Purpose? You mean to destroy the US military? What then?"

"Whatever he tells me."

Oliver nodded. "I see. You're his lapdog. Does he give you treats when you do the right thing? Does he pat your head and tell you what a good fucking boy you've been?"

Finally, there was a crack in Daniel's mask. He took three large steps forward, placing himself beside Hylar. Anger deformed his features. "I'm not his lapdog, I'm his *soldier*. This man gave me unrivaled abilities. He made me what I am today, and if he tells me to fight, then I fight. If he tells me to take over the whole goddamn country, then that's what I'll do."

Hylar placed a hand on Daniel's shoulder. "Calm. Oliver's merely trying to get a rise out of you. He knows his freedom has come to an end. He knows Tori's future is bleak. He's desperate."

Oliver crossed his arms over his chest. "Tori will survive this. I'll be free. You'll both be ten feet underground. That's what I know."

Hylar shook his head. "Wrong." He took a small step forward. "You want to know the master plan? Here it is. New soldiers will be created. The second the new shipment of drugs arrives in the country, we get to work creating more of you. Then, breeding experiments will start. Boys will be raised as soldiers. Ultimate weapons."

Oliver tried not to balk at the danger the world would be in if that came to pass.

A small smile touched Hylar's lips. "My army will be rebuilt. It will be unstoppable. You'll be part of that army, whether you want to be or not. We're going to decimate the US military. Together."

CHAPTER 26

From her peripheral vision, Samantha watched as Daniel moved forward, stopping to stand beside Hylar.

Oliver had understood. He'd gotten rid of the eyes watching her.

Now she had to act.

Samantha's fingers moved quickly over the keyboard. She could move them much faster, but she didn't. The possibility of giving herself away was too great. Of alerting her captors that she was no longer doing what she was supposed to.

She didn't need much time. A minute, tops. But who knew how long the men would be distracted?

Samantha had taken a cyber security course at university, never actually thinking she would need to use any of it. It was there she'd learned about certain security flaws…ones that allowed attackers to leverage Bluetooth connections and take control of devices.

That's what she intended to do now.

She'd detected the Bluetooth signal less than an hour ago. Someone in the area had left it on. She wasn't sure who. Hell, it might even be someone in another building. Someone unconnected to all of this.

She didn't care. She had it—and she could use it.

God, she was glad she had a near photographic memory. Usually, it meant she remembered *too* much. Useless information she'd never use. Right now, it meant she could recall the coding commands.

Opening a command prompt window, Samantha typed the first code: "hci scan".

Immediately, "scanning" appeared on the screen.

It took a few seconds for the sequence to appear: 00:0A:4T:7S:27:33.

Yes! That was the Bluetooth address for the device.

Samantha quickly initiated the pairing of her computer to the device and switched on interactive mode. Sweat beaded her forehead.

She was in. She had full control over the phone.

Speedily, Samantha typed in a line of code to retrieve the GPS coordinates of the phone's location. It didn't take long. Once she had that, she typed the last command—the one that allowed her to send an email to Marble Protection. It was an email address she'd memorized the day Tori had accepted the mission from Hylar.

Samantha punched in the coordinates and hit send.

Once it was done, she pressed the command to delete the email from the sent folder. Then, before anyone noticed, she disconnected the device from the computer.

Done.

Her heart rate was slightly elevated, and her hands were clammy, but no one had turned to look at her. If they did notice she was slightly out of sorts, hopefully they'd assume it was from Hylar's words.

She shot a quick glance at Oliver. He wasn't looking at her, but she hoped by simply looking up, he would know she was done.

His team needed to be as good as Hylar described. That was the only way they'd defeat these guys. She didn't care about her own life; they'd already tortured her enough that nightmares would plague the rest of her days.

She couldn't let them kill Tori. The only person left in the world she cared about.

~

KYE RUBBED HIS EYES. He'd barely slept in the last twenty-four hours. Frustration gnawed at his insides. So did anger. And an overwhelming sense of being powerless.

Oliver and Tori had been taken right in front of him. And he hadn't been able to do a goddamn thing about it.

He scanned the laptop screen. Wyatt's laptop. The guy had been on it since they'd arrived back at Marble Falls. Searching for anything that could tell them where Oliver or Tori had been taken. Kye had managed to convince him to take a break. Shut his eyes for at least an hour.

The guy wouldn't be away long. Hell, he'd probably be back within the hour.

The team was scattered around Marble Protection. They'd used every resource they had to find the couple...business footage, street surveillance, airline bookings. They even had the CIA working on their end.

So far, they'd found nothing helpful.

Where are you, brother?

He could still see the desperation on Tori's face as she was carried out of that house. The memory haunted him. He hated that he hadn't been able to get to her. To save Tori or Oliver before they'd been taken outside.

Kye and Wyatt had been outnumbered. They were never

going to win that fight.

Footsteps neared the office moments before Bodie stepped into the room, taking a seat. "Anything?"

Kye shook his head, no words leaving his mouth.

His friend scrubbed a hand over his face. "This can't be happening."

"We'll find them." *We have to.*

"We can't lose them." Bodie's voice was tortured. As pained as the rest of them felt.

"We won't."

There was a brief silence before Bodie finally sighed. "What's next?"

Kye turned back to the screen. "Evie's out there with Luca, doing another search on Tori's friend Samantha. She thinks Hylar wiped her past, which is why we haven't found anything on her. I'm still searching through street surveillance."

He was just clicking out of a surveillance video when an email notification popped up on the screen. Kye clicked into it immediately. Maybe it was the CIA with a lead...

The contents made him frown. "What the hell?"

Bodie straightened. "What is it?"

"GPS coordinates." Literally just that. No words. No explanation. He did a quick Google search on the coordinates. "It's a location on the outskirts of Killeen, Texas. A multistory office building, to be exact."

Bodie pulled out his phone and sent a text. Seconds later, the entire team was in the room, as well as Evie.

Kye and Bodie were already standing, Wyatt taking Kye's place behind the screen. Evie moved to sit beside him, alternating between watching his screen and her own.

After a minute of typing, they both stopped, and Wyatt was on his feet. "It's Hylar."

Kye tensed. "How do you know?"

Wyatt was already moving toward the storage cupboard. Pulling out weapons.

It was Evie who answered. "The top five floors are being rented under the name of a Tanya Hoffman."

Tanya. Hylar's half-sister. A woman who'd been dead for months.

CHAPTER 27

*T*ori snuggled into the warm chest below her cheek. She didn't need to see to know who it belonged to. His familiar masculine scent gave him away.

Oliver.

Slowly, she opened her eyes. Oliver was shirtless, cradling her in his arms. When she looked down at her own body, she realized she was wearing his shirt.

When she tried to sit up, the ache in her abdomen stole her breath. From the belt and the high-voltage electricity that had coursed through not just her, but Oliver too.

At the memory, her hands went straight to his chest. Searching for injuries. There wasn't so much as a spot of redness. "Are you okay?"

How did he look so perfect?

"I'm fine, honey. I heal fast," Oliver murmured quietly, pushing some hair from her face. "Are *you* okay?"

Okay? No. She wouldn't say she was okay. But she was better than when she'd fallen asleep. The terror of what she'd been through, of what she'd watched *Oliver* go through, combined with him not waking, had been pure hell.

"I'm glad you're awake."

His arms tightened around her, but only slightly. She noticed that he was careful to avoid applying too much pressure to her side.

She looked toward the window to see rain falling. There wasn't much light. Whether that was because clouds were covering the sun or it was late afternoon, she wasn't sure.

Then she took in the rest of the room, immediately spotting Samantha.

Her friend shifted her gaze to Tori. She still looked sad. And tired. Still had ghosts in her eyes.

Tori tried to smile, but she couldn't. Her lips wouldn't work that way. Not when there was so little to smile about.

Her friend was so strong, withstanding torture, refusing to build the microchip for as long as she had...yet five minutes with Tori and she was going against everything she believed in. Because Tori asked her to.

She hoped she was right. That Oliver's team would find and save them. She *had* to be right.

The fact that they hadn't come yet, that Samantha was still in exactly the same spot as when Tori had fallen asleep, didn't fill her with hope.

"I'm sorry." Tori said the words quietly, but she was sure Samantha heard.

Samantha lifted a shoulder. "It was always going to end this way. They were going to make sure of it."

God, she hated them.

What did they plan to do to Samantha once she was finished? Kill her? Use Tori against her to create more? Would they force them both to watch Oliver become a robot?

Tori pressed herself tighter against Oliver's body. She was scared for him. For her friend. So damn scared.

When Samantha turned her attention back to her work, Tori looked up at Oliver. He didn't seem worried. But she knew the man was good at masking his emotions. Preventing her from seeing anything that would upset her.

"I don't want them to change you."

Some of the mask fell. "They won't. They can't."

Usually, trusting Oliver was easy. Right now, it was the hardest thing ever. Samantha was a genius. If anyone could create something that could make a person do things they wouldn't normally do, it was her.

Tori lifted a hand and touched his cheek. "Whatever happens, I want you to know—"

"Don't."

Tori frowned. There were things she needed him to hear.

He lowered his head, bringing his face closer to hers. "Anything you have to say, you can tell me once we're back home. Where evil isn't listening. We'll light candles, play your favorite music...we won't be sitting on a cold floor with electrified bars surrounding us."

The mention of electricity had a small shudder running up her spine.

Oliver's mouth thinned, his hand stroking her back. He placed his lips to her ear. "I'm sorry. I'm going to do everything in my power to make sure they don't hurt you again. We're going to get out of here."

She wanted to believe him. She really did. But the futility of the situation weighed on her. And what if she never got to say those words to him? "But if we don't—"

"We will."

He wasn't going to let her say it. But he knew.

If something happened, if one of them didn't make it out of this alive, he knew.

She pressed a kiss to his chest, right above his heart. A kiss that said I love you. A kiss she felt deep in her own heart. She lingered for a long time, feeling the beating of his heart against her lips.

It was only the sound of a door opening that had her glancing up. Hylar stepped into the room, followed by Carter. She stiffened her spine to keep from flinching. Daniel still stood in the corner.

Hylar walked straight toward Samantha, and Tori suddenly wanted to move across the room. Stand between her friend and danger and protect her.

Samantha, always so brave, didn't move or flinch.

He stopped beside her. "Is it ready?"

"Almost."

Tori felt the slight tightening of Oliver's arms around her. She didn't understand what he was trying to convey...until Carter chuckled.

"That was a lie."

Hylar grabbed Samantha by the neck and Tori shot to her feet. She'd only made it a single step before Oliver grabbed her and tugged her behind him.

"Take your hand off her," Oliver snarled, each word laced with hate.

Hylar didn't pay Oliver an ounce of attention. "Don't lie to me. It won't end well for you. Is it finished?"

He released her neck. Red marks in the form of fingerprints remaining on her flesh. Samantha's chest rose and fell a few times before she answered. "Yes."

No. Tori grabbed Oliver's arm. That meant they'd take him. She couldn't lose him!

"Good." Hylar stepped back and turned his gaze to Daniel. "Call the surgeon."

Daniel nodded before leaving the room.

Oliver scoffed. "You have a surgeon?"

Hylar smiled. "Most people can either be bought or threatened into doing what you want."

Tori wondered which category the surgeon fell into. Probably the latter.

Hylar didn't take his eyes off Carter as he spoke. "Get the tranquilizer."

Tori's chest tightened. This was it. The moment they'd be separated. Oliver would be taken and probably return as someone else. A stranger.

Less than a minute passed before Carter stepped back into the room.

Just as a distant bang sounded.

Carter stopped moving.

Hylar's brows pulled together. "What was that?"

Tori looked up at Oliver. His expression hadn't changed.

Adrien ran into the room, closely followed by Daniel and Kip. Adrien had a phone in his hand, which he held out to Hylar. "They found us. They're downstairs. Pete and Anthony are trying to hold them off."

Hylar's features twisted. "*No.*" He grabbed the phone from Adrien, disbelief distorting his features as he studied the screen. He shoved it back into the guy's hand before turning to Samantha.

He backhanded her, sending her to the floor.

Tori cried out. She tried to run forward, but Oliver stopped her once again.

Hylar towered over Samantha. "You stupid bitch! You did this, didn't you?"

Samantha pushed herself onto her elbows, blood running from her lip. Yet still, she smiled. "Yes."

Hylar's chest was heaving. He appeared to be caught between wanting to kill Samantha and running.

Run, asshole. See how far you get.

"My brothers are here," Oliver said quietly, everyone's attention shifting to him. "And they're going to make sure you breathe your last breath today, Hylar."

Now Tori saw real fear in the commander's eyes.

Suddenly, the room plunged into darkness, the only light

coming from what little remained outside. It wasn't much, but it was enough.

Before she could anticipate his next move. Oliver shot forward, grabbing the cage bars and yanking them apart. The metal groaned as it separated.

"Shoot him!" Hylar shouted.

Tori screamed as Carter lifted a gun. She expected to see Oliver drop to the floor.

He didn't. He remained standing, the small tranquilizer dart in hand.

Tori's mouth dropped open. He'd caught it.

Carter was raising the gun again when Oliver shot forward. Before he could reach him, Adrien hit Oliver from the side, the two powerful soldiers colliding and falling to the floor.

Violence erupted between them.

Carter seemed to be about to shoot again, while Kip and Daniel moved to help Adrien, but Hylar's words stopped all three of them.

"Daniel, Kip, go downstairs, help Anthony and Pete. Don't let them up. Text me when an exit is open." The two ran out of the room. Hylar turned to Carter. "Don't let anything happen to Samantha or the finished microchip."

Tori made eye contact with her friend. She lunged toward Samantha but Hylar intercepted her. Hands latching onto her upper arms, he yanked her back toward him.

Tori threw an elbow, nailing him in the gut. She spun, her fist flying forward, but he caught it. Hylar threw his own punch. The hit caught her right in the temple.

Her brain fogged as Hylar threw her over his shoulder and started moving. He stopped once he reached a stairwell and grabbed something from his pocket. His phone. There was a short pause before he cursed.

Her head pounded, but she was pretty sure she knew what

had just happened. Hylar realized his exits were cut off. His men were failing him. He had nowhere to run.

When he started up the stairs, Tori kicked and punched in an attempt to get free. Eventually nailing him hard enough that he cried out, dropping her to the steps.

Tori pushed up, preparing to run—when a sharp pain cut through her stomach.

She looked down to see a knife lodged in her gut.

Hylar pulled it out and blood began to spread across Oliver's shirt.

She tried to cover the wound but Hylar grabbed her, dragging her stumbling behind him.

She didn't fight. She could barely breathe through the haze of pain.

When they stepped onto the roof, she almost fell to the ground, dizziness intensifying. She barely noticed the rain soaking into her shirt or the cold air whipping across her face.

Hylar dragged her across the roof. If she hadn't been using every ounce of energy to remain conscious, to stay upright, she might have balked at the height. They had to be ten floors up. And they were standing right on the edge.

CHAPTER 28

Oliver caught the dart in his right hand.

When Carter lifted the gun again, Oliver was already running. There was no guarantee he'd catch the dart a second time.

Adrien's body collided with Oliver's before he could reach Carter, sending them both to the ground.

Even as his back hit the floor, he punched Adrien in the jaw. Then he threw another.

Oliver got three punches in before he heard a soft whimper from Tori.

Flinging his head up, he saw Hylar grab her, Tori struggling against him.

Oliver was on his feet in seconds.

Before he'd taken a step, something hard hit him in the head, throwing him to his knees. He looked around in time to see Adrien's fist coming at him again.

Oliver dodged the hit before tackling the man around the middle. He tried to end him quickly, but every hit was either blocked or followed up by a hit from Adrien of equal intensity.

At a hard blow to his face, Oliver fell to the floor, his vision blurring for a second. As his sight cleared, he caught Adrien reaching for something on his ankle. He didn't need twenty-twenty vision to know it was a weapon.

Oliver leapt forward, grabbing the hand that held the gun just as Adrien pulled the trigger. The gunshot echoed through the room, piercing the window.

Adrien kneed Oliver in the midsection, sending him backward. The asshole raised the gun again and Oliver heard gunfire.

Then saw blood dripping from a hole in Adrien's forehead.

His eyes went blank and his body dropped to the floor.

Oliver turned to see Asher lowering his gun. The rest of the team rushed in behind him. Luca held out a hand to help Oliver up. "Everyone's dead except Hylar and Carter."

Oliver swung his gaze around the room. "If the exits are blocked, Carter must still be here. Samantha, too. Hylar took Tori."

Kye stepped forward. "He must have taken her to the roof, because he didn't pass us on the way up. All floors below are clear of heartbeats."

"Red and I will search this floor for Carter and Samantha," Eden said, already moving. "The rest of you go up."

Oliver took off toward the stairs. Kye shoved a gun into his hand on the way.

They moved quickly. When Oliver reached the roof, his feet came to an abrupt stop.

There was no sign of Carter or Samantha—but Hylar held Tori against his body as a shield. A gun was pressed to her head as they stood on the ledge of the building.

He scanned her body, immediately spotting the blood soaking through her shirt. Everything in him went cold. Blood roared in his ears.

The asshole had stabbed her. Oliver would tear the guy's heart out for that.

His teammates stood beside him. "It's over, Hylar. Let her go."

Water beat down, soaking them. Cold air whipping their skin. Hylar shook his head. "It can't be over."

There was panic in the guy's eyes. So much more than Oliver had ever seen before.

For the first time, Hylar realized he wasn't going to win. He was going to die and never get his revenge.

Oliver felt just as panicked as Hylar looked. All it would take was one step backward...one slip. "Let. Her. Go."

Hylar visibly tightened his grip on Tori's throat. "You boys could have held the world in the palm of your hands. You threw it away! Now you'll live out your worthless lives as *nothing!*"

Footsteps sounded from the stairs seconds before Eden and Bodie joined their brothers.

Oliver's gaze remained on Tori's. *It will be okay, baby.*

"You wanted to create killing machines," Mason shouted over the rain. "You did. We're *exactly* what you designed us to be. We just never had the same agenda as you."

"You're weak!" Hylar spat. "I should have identified that weakness and destroyed you. A stupid mistake."

"No." Asher spoke almost quietly. "Your mistake was underestimating what we'd do to keep each other safe. The lengths we'd go to protect the people we love."

"Those feelings and relationships," Eden added, "they're the reason we're here, and you're there."

Wyatt inched forward. "The second you declared war on us, you signed your own death certificate."

A maniacal-sounding laugh released from Hylar. "You think I'm scared of death? Most of me died back in South Sudan. I welcome it!" When the corners of his mouth lifted, dread uncoiled in Oliver's gut. He readied his body to leap forward. "But you? You all *fear* it. Fear one of your own dying. So this is only fair, isn't it? You destroyed my chance at revenge. So I destroy your brotherhood."

The gun swung toward Oliver.

He was already dodging the bullet when Tori's arm swung, pushing up the hand that held the gun.

Hylar's body jerked…feet slipping on the wet surface…

Sending them both backward, over the side of the ten-story building.

∼

EVERY INCH of Tori's body was shaking. From the cold. The blood loss. The muzzle of the gun pushing into her skull.

There was no scenario where she saw herself surviving this. Either Hylar was shot or shoved off the building, pulling her down with him, or Hylar shot *her*.

Either way, she dies.

The men spoke around her, but she paid no attention to what was being said. Her entire focus was on Oliver. When his gaze finally shifted from the gun to her eyes, his face softened. She knew what he was trying to do. Comfort her with a look. Let her know that he'd save her.

God, she wished she could talk to him. Speak those words she hadn't been allowed earlier.

At least he would survive this. He wouldn't be turned into a monster. He wouldn't be used to murder innocent people.

They had Hylar. And he would die.

When the hand around her throat tightened, a soft whimper escaped. It was swallowed by the storm that raged around her.

Mason said something. He sounded fierce. He *looked* fierce. They all did. Like an army.

Thunder boomed to the right. It didn't pull a single person's attention. Mother Nature was violent but insignificant right now.

Wyatt inched forward. "The second you declared war on us, you signed your own death certificate."

She felt the tensing of Hylar's muscles.

"You think I'm scared of death? Most of me died back in South Sudan. I welcome it!" He paused. The pressure of the gun against her head lessened. "But you? You all *fear* it. Fear one of your own dying. So this is only fair, isn't it? You destroyed my chance at revenge. So I destroy your brotherhood."

The words had barely left his mouth before Tori knew—one of the men in front of her was going to die.

If it was Oliver, it would destroy her. If it was one of his brothers, it would destroy *him*.

She couldn't let that happen.

The moment the gun left her head, Tori's arm swung, pushing the hand holding the weapon into the air.

Then they were falling backward. Air rushing past her face.

Everything happened so quickly.

His hand releasing her.

Hylar grabbing the building.

Tori grabbing his ankle.

She dug her fingers in, frantic to hang on. His other leg shot out to kick her off. It almost worked. Almost. Tori's fingers were too tenacious. Her desperation to live too great.

Ignoring the screaming pain from her stomach wound, Tori dug her nails into his flesh.

She didn't look down. She couldn't. She used all her focus to hold on to the man who literally held their lives in his hand.

Thunder rumbled through the air. She looked up to see that Hylar's hold on the edge of the roof slipping.

Tori sucked in a breath—just as a hand from above latched onto Hylar.

Oliver.

His head popped over the edge. He pulled Hylar onto the roof easily, throwing him to the side. Then he grabbed Tori, crushing her to his chest.

Relief. Shock. Utter exhaustion. It all hit Tori like a freight train. Her entire body trembled as she lay in the arms of the man she loved.

Suddenly, a gunshot sounded.

Oliver's body jolted. He let out a grunt.

Before she had a chance to look up, there was a second gunshot.

Tori spotted Kye, gun in hand. Her gaze went to Hylar next. He lay on the ground with a bullet wound to his head. His eyes open and blank. The small gun he must have pulled from a hidden holster laying by his side.

She didn't have time to be shocked at the man's death—because Oliver was falling. His body crumbling to the roof.

Oh god. He'd been shot!

Blood spread from beneath him, confirming he'd been hit in the back.

Tori screamed, hands going to his chest. His cheek. "Oliver! Oh Jesus…Oliver! Open your eyes. Please open your eyes!"

Strong hands grabbed her arms, pulling her away. She cried out. Fighting the person who was separating her from Oliver.

He lay there so still. The normally powerful man now limp.

She struggled against Kye's unyielding hold as the rest of the team went to Oliver. They applied pressure to the wound before lifting him.

Kye lowered his mouth to her ear. "Stop fighting me, Tori. We need to get Oliver out of here. He needs medical attention."

Tori's body immediately wilted. He was right. There was nothing she could do.

She sobbed silently as Kye negotiated his way down the stairs. She swore he asked her some questions. Maybe about her injuries. She barely heard him. Just like how she barely felt the pain of her wounds. Her body was numb. Oliver could be dying right now…he could be dead.

A sob escaped her throat and tears slipped down her cheeks.

If he died, it was her fault. He'd died saving her. His death would be something she would never recover from.

CHAPTER 29

*T*ori's eyes threatened to close but she refused to let them. She was tired—no, she was exhausted—but she needed to remain awake for when Oliver finally opened his eyes.

He still hadn't regained consciousness. Her normally strong and fierce man, so still beneath the sheets.

Sage was the only doctor who had attended him. She'd said the bullet had narrowly missed his heart, but he'd lost blood. A lot of it.

Luckily, Asher and Bodie were both the same blood type and were able to donate. Sage had done everything in her power to save him. Now it was up to Oliver.

At the sound of the door opening, Tori scrubbed away any residual wetness on her cheeks. She'd cried a lot of tears; it would only take one look at her to see that. Still, she felt the need to dry her cheeks.

A hand touched her shoulder. "How are you doing, Tori?"

Kye. Of course it was. The man had been amazing since carrying her from the building. He'd remained by her side most of the time and ensured she had access to Oliver.

"Sage says he should wake soon—"

"No." Kye kneeled beside her. "How are *you* doing?"

Her? She was exhausted. Drained in every way possible. And so scared for the man she loved. "Physically, I barely feel where they stitched up the knife wound. Emotionally, I feel guilty. Sad. Angry."

And so much more.

Kye placed a comforting hand on her knee. "I feel all those things too. We've never come so close to losing one of our own."

Tori could see the shadows under the man's eyes. The strain on his face. He looked like he was only just keeping his emotions in check.

"What's keeping me going," Kye continued, "is knowing he'll be okay. Because he will. Every time I walk in here, his heart is beating a little stronger. There's more color to his face. Our boy's strong. He's going to survive this."

Oliver *was* strong. The strongest man she knew.

Leaning over, she hugged Kye, so grateful to the man for keeping her sane the last twelve hours. "Thank you."

When Kye pulled away, he gave her a small smile. "I'm gonna get home for some rest. Luca just arrived and is in the hall if you need anything."

She nodded. She wasn't surprised the guy didn't try to convince her to go back to Oliver's home and get some rest too. He knew she wouldn't.

He was just turning when she touched his arm. She'd asked him this question already...but maybe this time, his answer would change. "Any luck finding Samantha?"

He sighed, and she already knew. "No. Not yet. But we will."

Tori bit the inside of her cheek to stop the disappointment from showing. If anyone could find her, it was these guys. She needed to have faith.

Nodding, she watched Kye leave before turning back to Oliver. She lifted his hand in both of hers. "There's something I never told you." Tori stroked her thumb back and forth over his knuckles, feeling every indent and scar. "I fell for you long before I was ready to tell you I did. If I'm being honest, it was probably after our first night together. It's crazy. I know it is. Falling for a stranger. I remember thinking it was just attraction. It would fade when I drove home. It didn't."

She swallowed, her fingers moving to the veins on his hand.

"I tried so hard to stay detached that day. To view you as a job, not a man who set my heart to racing. You made it impossible. With your smile. Your humor. Your light touches that made me crazy. Every time your body grazed mine, my skin felt like it was burning up."

That was something that hadn't changed.

"When I finally decided to trust my gut, to trust *you*, it was like a weight had been lifted off my chest. My plan was to return to you. Convince you that I was someone worth dating." Her finger touched a scar that ran diagonally across his hand. "I was afraid though. I knew you were a bachelor. I wondered if I would be enough to convert you to a relationship guy. Enough for you to take a chance on."

What would have happened if she hadn't developed amnesia? If she hadn't needed Oliver's protection? Would he still have spent time getting to know her?

"You're more than enough..."

At the sound of Oliver's voice, Tori's eyes shot to his face. He was awake. His green eyes open and looking directly at her.

The hand she'd just been stroking lifted, touching her cheek. "You've been crying."

She tried to smile, but it was wonky as hell. "I was so worried!"

Oliver's hand curved around her cheek. Tori immediately leaned her face into his touch. "I was always coming back to you, Tori."

She held his wrist with both hands. Turning her head, she pressed a kiss into his palm. "Thank you."

For protecting her. Coming back to her. For everything.

"You don't need to thank me, honey." His thumb stroked her cheek, wiping away a tear she hadn't realized had dropped. "How long have I been unconscious?"

Too long. "About twelve hours. The bullet just missed your heart, but you lost a lot of blood. You got a transfusion with Asher and Bodie's blood."

"Ah, it's good to have brothers."

When Oliver sat up, Tori immediately leaned forward, about to attempt to stop him. Her quick movement caused a shot of pain to her knife wound. She ignored it. "Oliver, what are you doing? You need to rest."

No pain or discomfort crossed his features. "I feel fine. I wouldn't be surprised if the wound is just about healed." His brows pulled together as he scanned her midsection. "How are you?"

"I'm okay."

He gave a soft growl at her quick response. With strength he shouldn't be using, Oliver lifted her onto his lap.

"Your injuries—"

"I told you. I'm fine." Once she was across his legs, his hand returned to her cheek. "How are you feeling?"

About the knife wound? The gun to her head? The fall off a ten-story building? Or about seeing him get hurt?

"I'm okay."

Mostly, she just couldn't get that moment out of her head. When she realized he was bleeding out on the roof and wasn't getting up.

He was silent as he studied her face. "You're a warrior, Tori. So strong and brave. And god, do I love you."

Her heart fluttered at his words. The smile she'd been unable to fully form moments before now touching her lips. "I love you, too." She cradled his face with her hands. "I was so worried that you'd never hear me say those words."

He shook his head. "Nothing was going to stop me."

He dipped his head and kissed her. The weight of the last few days suddenly felt a bit lighter. The heartache, the uncertainty, faded.

In Oliver, she found refuge.

~

"I CAN'T BELIEVE he's dead."

Oliver lifted his beer to his lips. Bodie's words held the ring of disbelief that each man on the team felt.

Luca nodded. "It doesn't feel real."

It really didn't. It was difficult to put into words what Hylar finally being gone meant to them. A huge weight had been lifted off Oliver's chest. He could breathe again.

His eyes sought out Tori. They were at AJ's Bar. She was sitting on a stool with the rest of the women surrounding her while Oliver sat in a booth with Mason, Bodie, and Luca.

Her smile was almost convincing. No one would see the strain behind it…except him.

"It's been a week since he died," Oliver said quietly. "Yet we haven't located Carter or Samantha."

And it was killing Tori. Carter had managed to escape, taking Tori's best friend with him.

Mason ran a hand through his hair. "The asshole must have gotten past us somehow."

The storm had been loud. It wouldn't have been that hard for someone with Carter's abilities.

"Why would he take her?" Bodie asked, frowning. "As far as we know, he has no more men. No resources. You'd need both to achieve what Hylar was trying to accomplish."

Luca lifted a shoulder. "Maybe he plans to sell what Samantha created."

Oliver ground his teeth at the thought. Any chip that could

control a person's actions, take away their free will, should not be in existence. "It's killing Tori," he said quietly. "The women are like sisters. Tori hasn't said it, but I know that she feels guilty that she got out and Samantha didn't."

He wished he could reassure her that they'd find her friend, but there was no way he could guarantee that. There was a very real possibility that once Carter realized his team was gone, that Hylar had died, he'd kill her.

Oliver watched as the women laughed at something. Tori smiled. It was like she couldn't muster a laugh.

Damn Project Arma. The program was still messing with people, even after it was over.

Pushing his beer away, Oliver stood and headed over to his woman. He didn't say anything as he gently pulled her away from the group. He wrapped his arms around her and moved gently to the music. Tori rested her head on his chest.

"I'm sorry she's still missing."

Her arms tightened around him. "You don't need to say sorry. I know you and the guys are doing everything you can to find her."

They were, but dammit, it wasn't enough.

He lowered his mouth to her ear. "Have I told you how beautiful you look in that dress?" The woman was always beautiful. But tonight, in her tight black dress, he was having a tough time taking his eyes off her.

"You have. Multiple times, actually. But you can say it a hundred more times and I'll never tire of hearing it."

"You're beautiful." He pushed his nose into her hair. There was something else he wanted to tell her. Something he should wait to say, but he couldn't. He wanted to see a real smile on her face tonight. "Tomorrow, I have a surprise for you."

She looked up at him. "A surprise?'

Gently, he pushed some hair behind her ear. "I was going to

wait to tell you, but I'm a selfish man and I want to see you happy."

He hated the pain in her eyes. Hopefully, this would bring some of the light back.

"We found Charlie."

Tori stopped moving. Her mouth opening and voice softening. "What?"

"I asked Evie to look into it. A hiker found Charlie wandering through the national forest the afternoon you were taken to the hospital. He's been with the guy who found him ever since. We're going to drive down and pick him up tomorrow."

Tori was silent. Her eyes studied him like she was trying to work out whether to believe him or not. Then she buried her head in his chest.

"Thank you." Her words were so quiet, they almost got drowned in the music. "Thank you so, so much."

He hugged her tighter, at the same time being careful of her healing knife wound. "I'm glad he's okay, honey."

Tori had told him how much Charlie meant to her. He'd been her mother's dog and was a daily reminder of her mother's love. Oliver was glad he could help ease some of Tori's pain.

They remained on the dance floor for a while, swaying to the music and just holding each other. It wasn't until his phone rang from his pocket that he finally stopped.

Oliver pressed a kiss to her head. "I'll be back, I'm just going to answer this." Stepping away, he answered the call. "Cage. What's going on?"

"I've got a tail."

Oliver tensed, quickly returning to the booth where his brothers sat. "Where are you?"

"Driving home from Marble Protection. They're—" Kye suddenly cursed through the line.

Dread filled Oliver's gut. "What is it?"

Mason, Luca, and Bodie stood.

"They're not trying to remain hidden anymore." Kye's voice was raised. The sound of his car engine loud. "Fuck, they're fast!"

Mason whipped his phone out. "I'll track the GPS on his phone."

There was more cursing on the line, followed by a loud bang.

"What was that?"

Mason and Luca started moving toward the exit. Bodie remained with Oliver.

Kye took a second to answer. "The asshole hit my car with his. I think he's going to—"

Glass shattering echoed through the line. Then the sound of tires squealing.

Another bang. Louder than the one before.

"Cage? Talk to me."

There was silence.

Oliver's heart raced as he listened for something...anything.

There was the sound of metal scraping metal. Like the car door was being pulled off.

The line went dead.

Oliver swore under his breath. "I'll follow Eagle and Rocket."

Bodie nodded, looking as grim as Oliver felt. "I'll stay with the women."

Oliver raced outside and jumped into his car. He brought up the tracking software, immediately locating Kye's phone. Oliver hadn't been driving long when Mason's call came through.

"Are you with him?" Oliver's words were rushed.

"He's gone."

He pressed his foot harder on the accelerator. No, that wasn't possible. "He can't be. I'm almost there."

Oliver hung up. Refusing to believe it. A couple minutes later, he stopped behind Kye's crashed vehicle and jumped out.

His feet came to a quick stop beside Mason and Luca. The car was in bad shape. One of the back tires was flat, the back window was smashed, and the car had hit a tree hard. The driver's door had been pulled off the vehicle and there was blood splatter on the seat.

Mason was right. Kye was gone.

If Oliver had to hazard a guess, he'd say someone had shot something through the back window, hitting Kye in the neck or shoulder. Once the car crashed, they'd taken him.

CHAPTER 30

*K*ye roused slowly.

Damn, his head was pounding. It felt like a jackhammer was going to work up there. Hitting at his skull, hard and unrelenting.

He lifted a hand to his neck. The skin was warm and sensitive. Something had pricked him.

No. Not just something. He'd felt this pain before.

He'd been tranquilized. Again.

His eyes shot open. Tension slammed into his gut when he was greeted with prison bars.

What the hell?

He scanned the small space. The back wall was solid concrete, the other three walls metal bars. A small toilet sat in the corner, with a tap beside it. The floor was also cold concrete.

He barely felt it, but had he been a normal person, he knew he'd be damn well freezing.

Slowly, Kye stood, clenching his jaw. Someone had shot him. Taken him. Caged him.

Who?

He needed to know so he could murder the asshole.

He studied the space outside his cage. Three more cells, each sharing bars with the one beside it. All identical in size.

Outside the cells, there was open space and a door. There was also a camera in the corner of the room, near the ceiling.

Where the hell was he and who was watching him?

He tried to listen. Hear something, anything, outside this prison cell. He heard nothing. Not a damn thing. The walls had to be soundproof.

Bit by bit, the previous night came back to him. Driving home from his workout at Marble Protection. Spotting someone tailing him. Calling Oliver.

The asshole in the car must have shot the window out and gotten him with a tranquilizer. He touched a hand to his forehead, feeling the already healing cut from hitting the side window.

The anger expanded in his chest. Consuming him.

Kye was almost certain he knew who was responsible. Carter. It had to be.

As far as Oliver was aware, Carter was the last remaining member of Project Arma. Hylar was dead. Hylar's men, Carter's team, all dead...there was no one else.

Kye took note of the fact he was still wearing the sweatpants and tank top from last night. His shoes and socks were missing.

Other than the pounding head and sore neck, everything else felt okay. God, his head hadn't pounded this hard the last two times he'd been tranquilized.

Walking over to the bars, he inspected them with caution. What was the likelihood they were electrified?

Only one way to find out.

Reaching out, Kye touched a bar with one finger. Nothing. Slowly, he wrapped his right hand around it. Again, there wasn't so much as a shock.

Kye grabbed another bar with his left hand. Using every ounce of his strength, he attempted to pull the bars apart.

Goddammit. There was no give. What the hell were they made of?

Dropping his hands, he looked back up at the camera. Was Carter watching him right now? Was he smiling at his success?

Smile all you want, jerk. I won't be here for long.

Suddenly, the door to the room opened. The exact person he'd been expecting to see walked in.

Carter.

Kye clenched his fists, already wanting to rip the guy to pieces. He hated him with the same fire and intensity as he'd hated Hylar. The two men were cut from the same cloth.

Oliver looked to the woman he pulled behind him. Average height, about five foot seven. Blond curls pulled up into a hairband. Delicate looking. Fragile, even.

The woman had to be Tori's friend Samantha. He'd never seen a picture of her, but Tori had described her enough for him to guess.

The woman's sky-blue eyes met his. There was sadness there. Deep shadows under her eyes. From her experiences at their hands or pure exhaustion?

Probably both.

There was also the slightest hint of hope.

Hope because Kye was here?

Good. Because one way or another, he planned to get them both out.

Kye took in the bruise on her left temple. The way she favored her right leg, and the way Carter's fingers dug into her slender left arm.

Son of a bitch.

"You're finally awake," Carter said, unlocking the cell beside Kye's with his other hand.

"I am. So how about you stop manhandling the woman and pick on someone your own size."

Carter chuckled before yanking the door open and shoving

her inside. Samantha fell to the ground, a soft cry escaping her lips.

Kye growled. Fucking animal.

"Already wanting to save the damsel in distress." Carter locked the door to her cage before stepping in front of Kye.

The asshole was so close. If those damn bars weren't in the way, Kye would murder him. And he'd enjoy every second of it.

As if reading Kye's mind, Carter took a step forward, taunting him. "Bet you're thinking about how much you'd love to tear me to shreds right now."

Spot on. "If you didn't have me in a cage, you'd be dead."

Less than a minute. That was all he needed.

"But I *do* have you in a cage. And oh, how sweet it was to shoot you. Watch you crash right into that fucking tree."

Kye wrapped his fingers around the bars again. "So why didn't you kill me?"

"I may *want* you dead, but not enough to destroy you. Not in the way you think, anyway."

What did that mean? "What are you talking about?"

"You'll find out soon enough." Carter stepped back. His gaze shot over to Samantha. "I'll be back."

Kye clenched the bars harder as Carter exited the room. He wanted to scream at the guy to come back. To open his damn cage and fight him, man to man.

But there was no point. Carter was going to play this out his way.

It wasn't until the door slammed shut that Kye turned to look at the woman. Whereas his cell was devoid of any sleeping materials, she had a thin mattress—if you could even call it that—an old pillow and a sheet. It didn't look close to being enough to keep her warm.

She wore leggings and a sweatshirt, both of which were dirty. Like the woman had been wearing them for weeks, if not months.

She curled up beneath the sheet, her eyes already shutting.

He inched closer. "Tired?"

Her eyes didn't open. "I haven't slept in days. I was falling asleep while I was working. It's the only reason he brought me back here."

Her voice was soft and silky. He had an overwhelming urge to go to her. Wrap her in his arms and keep her safe. He gave himself a mental shake at the thought. His protective instincts were kicking into overdrive. He hated it when women weren't treated right.

"Why haven't you slept, honey?"

Her eyes opened, presumably at the endearment. "Carter's been forcing me to work nonstop."

Kye crouched in front of her. The mattress was right against the metal bars. If he reached his arm through, he could touch her. He needed to let her sleep...but he had to know. "What are you working on?"

She blinked slowly a couple of times. She was trying to keep her eyes open but struggling. "Are you one of Oliver's teammates?"

Teammate. Brother. The guy was family. "Yeah, I am. My name is Kye."

He expected her to introduce herself. She didn't. Her brows pulled together, worry glazing her eyes. "I'm sorry."

A lock of hair fell into her face. His hand twitched with the need to reach over and push it back. "What are you sorry about?"

"About what I created. I tried to fix it by destroying my work. I tried to withstand the torture..." She swallowed. "But I'm tired. When Tori asked me to do it... I can't keep fighting them."

Kye's body stiffened at the word torture. What had they done to her? What methods had they used to put those shadows under her eyes?

"It's okay."

None of this was okay. But he wanted to take some of her pain away. He felt like he *needed* to.

She shook her head. "Carter's forcing me to code the program again. When that's done, the chips will be recreated. Used on men like you."

Why? Why would Carter want to recreate Hylar's work? He didn't have a team anymore. Was he attempting to continue Hylar's fight? And if so, why?

"I'm not scared." He really wasn't. He had faith that either his team would get him out or he'd find a way to escape. Either way, Carter wouldn't be getting what he wanted.

For a moment, she was silent. Her gaze boring into his with a new intensity. When she spoke, there was a light tremble in her voice. "You *should* be scared. If they get a chip into you, you'll be at his mercy. You won't have free will. If he tells you to kill, you'll kill. No one will be safe."

Then it was obvious what had to happen. "They won't get it into me. Or my brothers."

He felt the second part was worth adding. Because he knew that was what Hylar had wanted. For his entire team to be controlled.

"I hope not." Samantha sighed and closed her eyes. "For the sake of you, your family...and everyone else."

Order Kye today!

ALSO BY NYSSA KATHRYN

PROJECT ARMA SERIES

Uncovering Project Arma

Luca

Eden

Asher

Mason

Wyatt

Bodie

Oliver

Kye

JOIN my newsletter and be the first to find out about sales and new releases -

https://www.nyssakathryn.com/vip-newsletter

ABOUT THE AUTHOR

Nyssa Kathryn is a romantic suspense author. She lives in South Australia with her daughter and hubby and takes every chance she can to be plotting and writing. Always an avid reader of romance novels, she considers alpha males and happily-ever-afters to be her jam.

Don't forget to follow Nyssa and never miss another release.

Facebook | Instagram | Amazon | Goodreads

DEC ·· ·· 2022

CPSIA information can be obtained
at www.ICGtesting.com
Printed in the USA
BVHW071942220222
629775BV00001B/189

9 780648 946267